Outbreak at Safe Harbor

Dr David R Madenberg

WESTBOW
PRESS
A DIVISION OF THOMAS NELSON

All bible quotations used in this book are taken from the New King James Version, Copyright 1982 by Thomas Nelson, Inc.

WestBow Press books may be ordered through booksellers or by contacting:

WestBow Press
A Division of Thomas Nelson
1663 Liberty Drive
Bloomington, IN 47403
www.westbowpress.com
1-(866) 928-1240

ISBN: 978-1-4497-0486-5 (sc)
ISBN: 978-1-4497-0485-8 (e)

Library of Congress Control Number: 2010939516

Printed in the United States of America

WestBow Press rev. date: 11/30/2010

Acknowledgments

I wish to express my deepest appreciation to all my loved ones and friends, whose assistance with the completion of this project proved invaluable.

To my wife and best friend, Heidi, whose prayers, patience, understanding, and advice were incalculable. To her, I give my everlasting love, devotion, and respect.

To Courtney, Devin, and Joshua, my children, whom I have watched over the years grow into devoted followers of Christ, I give my love and affection.

To my dear friends Pastor Isaiah VanHullum and Michael Landsgaard, my sincere appreciation for their patience and support.

To my mother-in-law and a tenacious prayer warrior, Mrs. Ana Stan, my profound gratitude and respect.

To my dad, Martin, my heartfelt love and appreciation. I pray that he, along with other family members, will one day come to know Jesus as their Messiah.

And to our Heavenly Father and Lord Jesus, my eternal gratitude, love, devotion, and obedience unto eternity.

Prologue

This book may prove offensive to some readers. Whereas some may consider the contents theologically inaccurate, others may be in complete agreement with what is written. My intent, however, is not to offend. It is to, rather, open the eyes of those who think because Christians are saved by grace, God holds us harmless for disobedient behavior. Many believers declare all that is required is to ask God for His forgiveness. Then, no consequences will be incurred for actions in violation of what is written in the Holy Bible.

As you read *Outbreak at Safe Harbor*, decide for yourselves whether consequences will befall even a believer whose behavior is contrary to the Word of God.

CHAPTER ONE

It was a balmy late June evening in the quaint town of Clarion, Wisconsin. The stars were twinkling as diamonds across a seemingly endless black sky. The moon was full, casting its majestic shadow through a wisp of clouds onto the lake adjacent to Clarion General Hospital.

In the Emergency Department of the hospital, Dr. Steven Talbott was in the process of discharging his remaining patient. "You'll do fine, Becky," he said, while writing a prescription for Becky's antibiotic. "Your sinus infection will improve in a day or two. Just be sure to take the medication for the full ten days."

"Okay, Dr. Talbott, and thanks for your help." Becky was one of Clarion's college students home for the summer. After she left, Dr. Talbott poured himself a cup of black coffee. He strolled out of the brightly illuminated ER through the ambulance entrance. He yearned for a short break between patients to enjoy the repose of the summer evening. As he exited through the heavy security door into the night, he could immediately feel the warm summer breeze blow gently across his face and through his neatly combed gray-streaked hair. He heard the familiar sound of crickets chirping as he gazed at the moonlight dancing upon the tiny rippling waves of nearby Clarion Lake. The scent of jasmine growing a few yards from the ER entrance permeated the night air, filling his nostrils with a sweet fragrance. It was almost midnight, and Dr. Talbott's shift ran from 8:00 PM to 8:00 AM. He was accustomed to the often-grueling hours inherent in the practice of emergency medicine, having been an ER physician for nearly three decades. Dr. Talbott thoroughly enjoyed practicing medicine in Clarion. He had moved there from a large metropolitan area after completing his medical training. The town eventually became a part of him. Residents of Clarion respected Dr. Talbott as a physician and considered him a friend. He was a member of Clarion's First Evangelical Church and made every attempt to put his faith into practice, whether in or out of the hospital. He was a dedicated Christian.

As the doctor embraced the peaceful solitude of the late evening, its silence was abruptly broken by the all too familiar blare of the ambulance radio. "Paramedic Unit Seven to Clarion General."

"Go ahead, Unit Seven, this is Clarion General," responded Marisa Jeffords, one of the two nurses on duty and a ten-year veteran of the ER.

"Clarion, this is Paramedic Unit Seven en route to your facility with a forty-five-year-old woman from Safe Harbor Bible Camp. At this time, she is complaining of severe abdominal cramping." Safe Harbor is a well-known Christian Bible camp located five miles west of Clarion, encircled by a forest and several small farms. Active only during the summer, the camp is visited by Christian families from all over the Midwest. "Clarion," the paramedics continued, "The patient informs us her abdominal pain began a couple of hours ago. She also states she has been experiencing profuse vomiting and diarrhea."

"Unit Seven, what are your patient's vital signs?" Marisa inquired.

"Clarion, the patient's blood pressure is 75/50, pulse is 130 and thready. Her respirations are 28, and the pulse oximeter reading is 95 percent on 3 liters of oxygen by nasal cannula."

From these vital signs, Marisa, one of the unit's most competent nurses, concluded the patient was in shock from dehydration, presumably due to the large amount of vomiting and diarrhea. "Unit Seven, does the patient respond to you verbally?" she asked.

"Clarion, the patient was initially unresponsive. We administered a liter of normal saline intravenously, and the patient is now beginning to talk to us. We are in the process of starting a second IV in her other arm," the paramedic replied.

"Ten-four, Unit Seven. What is your ETA?"

"Uh, Clarion, our ETA is approximately eight minutes."

"Unit Seven, keep pushing fluids and keep us informed of any changes in the patient's condition. Upon your arrival, please go directly to Exam Room Two."

"Ten-four, Clarion. We'll see you in about eight minutes. Unit Seven clear."

No sooner did Marisa replace the radio's handset than another call came in from a second paramedic unit. "Clarion General, Clarion General."

"This is Clarion General, Marisa responded.

"Clarion General, this is Paramedic Unit One en route from Safe Harbor Bible Camp with two patients, a mom and her daughter," the paramedic reported. "Patient One is a twenty-eight-year-old female, who is complaining of a severe headache and dizziness that started about two hours ago. She states she has no medical problems and does not take medication on a regular basis. Patient Two is a four-year-old female who began wheezing and is unable to stop coughing. Upon our arrival at Safe Harbor, we observed Patient Two extremely short of breath and barely able to verbalize. We administered an albuterol treatment and placed her on oxygen. The patient improved after the bronchodilator treatment. Patient Two's symptoms started about the same time Patient One began to experience her symptoms."

"Unit One, does Patient Two have a history of asthma?" Marisa asked.

"Negative, Clarion. Patient One tells us Patient Two does not have a history of asthma. Patient Two is normally healthy and does not take any meds."

"Unit One, thanks for your report. Keep us informed of any changes in either patient's condition," Marisa instructed. "Please take both patients to Exam Room Three upon your arrival."

"Ten-four, Clarion, Unit One clear."

As Marisa placed the handset back onto its cradle, Karen McMillian commented, "This is bizarre." Karen, the Emergency Department receptionist, had overheard both radio calls. "Safe Harbor opened for the summer just a week ago and we're already treating patients from there? Weird."

Before Marisa could respond, a family of three walked through the doors of the Emergency Department. As the trio approached the reception desk where Karen was seated, the head of the family introduced himself. "Hi, my name is Joshua Holstrom. This is my wife, Mary, and our daughter, Sara. We drove here from Safe Harbor Bible Camp."

"What seems to be the problem, Mr. Holstrom?" Karen inquired.

"Well, we just arrived at camp yesterday from Chicago. The three of us were fine when we got here, but about two hours ago, our ears began to ring. It's so loud, none of us can hear very well."

"It's crazy!" his wife Mary exclaimed. "We were all feeling just fine a couple of hours ago."

"Earlier tonight," Joshua continued, "I was talking with Alex Jensen. He arrived at Safe Harbor yesterday from St. Louis, along with his wife and children. While we were having supper together, Mr. Jensen mentioned that he and his family were starting to feel ill. They got so dizzy, they had to excuse themselves."

"As they got up, it looked like they were going to keel over!" Mary exclaimed, her arm around Sara's shoulders. The little girl looked scared.

"What do you think is going on?" Joshua asked.

"I'm not sure," Karen replied, "but we're going to get to the bottom of it!" With a confident smile, she turned to look for Derry White, the other nurse on duty. Derry was one of three nurses recently hired by Clarion General to work in the ER. Her slim, toned body and long jet-black hair made her easy to spot, and Karen waved at her. "Hey, Derry, could you come over here, please?"

By now, Unit Seven had checked in, and Marisa was occupied in Exam Room Two with the patient the paramedics had just brought in.

Derry smiled as she walked over to Karen and the Holstrom family. "Hi, I'm Derry. I'm one of the nurses on duty tonight. How can I help?" As Mr. Holstrom proceeded to retell his story to Derry, Paramedic Unit One arrived with their two patients. "Hi, guys, go to Exam Room Three," Derry instructed. "I'll be there shortly." She turned to Joshua and added, "Mr. Holstrom, would you mind taking your family to Exam Room Six, down the hall and to the right? Either Marisa or I will be with you soon."

To Karen she added, "Looks like it's going to be one of those busy summer nights in the ER! Would you let Dr. Talbott know we need him in Two?"

"Right away!" Karen replied. Derry hurried toward Exam Room Three, where Mom and daughter were awaiting medical attention. Before Karen could get up from her chair to summon Dr. Talbott, the telephone rang. "Good evening, Clarion General Hospital Emergency Department," Karen answered.

"Hello, this is Shelley Markham from Safe Harbor Bible Camp."

"Yes, ma'am. How can I help you?" Karen inquired.

"I'm one of the Safe Harbor camp nurses," Shelley stated. "I'm calling in regard to several people with me here in the camp dispensary."

"What seems to be the problem?"

"I have a family of six in the dispensary from Indiana," Shelley replied. "They arrived at Safe Harbor earlier today and were feeling well. Tonight, however, they are all experiencing severe muscle spasms throughout their bodies. They appear to be very uncomfortable and in quite a bit of pain. I would like to refer them to the ER so they can be examined by a physician."

"Could you please hold?" Karen asked the camp nurse. "Marisa or Derry, could one of you break free to take a phone call?" Karen urgently requested over the ER intercom. Just then, Dr. Talbott arrived at the reception desk. "Doctor," Karen said nervously while holding the telephone. "It's Shelley Markham from Safe Harbor. She's calling in regard to six more people over there who are ill. What is going on at that camp?" she questioned. As Karen and Dr. Talbott spoke, eight more people from Safe Harbor piled into the emergency department requesting medical attention.

They formed a line at the reception desk in front of Karen to register for treatment. It appeared these people did not know each other, and the symptoms they were describing seemed completely unrelated. Karen was nearing panic mode. By now, fourteen patients were in the ER from the camp, and they all required urgent treatment by Dr. Talbott, Marisa, and Derry. Dr. Talbott calmly took the telephone from Karen. "Hello, Shelley. This is Steve Talbott. What is going on at Safe Harbor tonight? We're inundated with patients from there. Has your husband been cooking the meals for these unfortunate people?" he asked jokingly. Shelley's husband, Pastor Jeremy Markham, and Steve Talbott had become good friends since Steve moved to Clarion to practice medicine thirty years earlier.

"Steve, I had no idea anyone else from Safe Harbor was sick," Shelley declared. "Are their conditions serious?"

"I don't know yet, Shelley," he replied. "I was just about to examine the first three who arrived by ambulance. We are in the process of evaluating fourteen patients from your camp, excluding the six who are with you in the dispensary. Please give me some time to examine these people. I won't be able to give you specific information because of the confidentiality issues, but I should be able to provide you with an idea as to what may be occurring there. Give me about an hour, and I'll get back to you. Oh, and Shelley," he added, "just a thought. Was the camp's well water checked for impurities prior to opening this year?"

"Yes and quite recently," she replied. "The health inspector assured us the water is free from contaminants. He specifically mentioned there was no evidence of pathogenic bacteria, toxic chemicals, or parasites. We have never had a problem with well water contamination," Shelley added. "And please, Steve, do let us know as soon as possible any information you are able to share. We love these people and also worry rumors may start to spread about some deadly plague engulfing Safe Harbor."

"I'll call you as soon as I know more," Steve said reassuringly. "And send those other six people over to us. It sounds as though they will require treatment along with the folks already here."

"Thanks Steve. I'll send them in the camp van as soon as possible."

As the two ended their conversation, Dr. Talbott handed the phone back to Karen. Replacing the receiver, Karen asked worriedly, "Dr. Talbott, what do you suppose is going on at Safe Harbor?"

"I don't know yet Karen, but I must admit it is very strange. In all my years practicing in Clarion," he stated somberly, "I have never seen or heard of anything like this occurring at the camp." With that, Dr. Talbott walked into Exam Room Two, where Marisa was attending to the patient with severe dehydration who had been brought in by the paramedics.

A middle-aged woman lay on the exam bed. She appeared weak and dehydrated. Stomach contents had gotten onto her clothing. Marisa removed the soiled garments, replacing them with a clean hospital gown. There was an IV running in each of the patient's arms, delivering life-saving fluids to replace those lost from vomiting and diarrhea. Dr. Talbott picked up the woman's medical chart. He wanted to review the information documented by the paramedics regarding her pre-hospital treatment. Her name was Allison Jeffries. "Hello, Allison, I'm Dr. Talbott, the emergency physician. How are you feeling now that the paramedics have given you some IV fluids?"

"I'm feeling a little better, Doctor, but still very queasy."

"Marisa, would you please give Allison Zofran four milligrams IV?" It should help alleviate Allison's nausea and vomiting.

"Right away doctor," Marisa replied as she left to retrieve the medication from the med room adjacent to the nurse's station.

Dr. Talbott thanked Marisa and sat down beside Allison. He began to ask her routine questions that help physicians diagnose certain conditions prior to performing the necessary physical examination. "Allison, do you have any medical problems or take any medications on a daily basis?"

"No, Doctor, I'm normally very healthy. I don't like taking even aspirin or acetaminophen," she replied. "But I do take multivitamins with calcium every day."

"Could you have accidentally ingested more than the prescribed dose?" Dr. Talbott asked.

"Absolutely not. I've been taking them for years and only one per day. I also work out regularly at least three or four times a week."

Dr. Talbott continued, "When did you arrive at Safe Harbor, and were you feeling ill before your arrival?"

"Well," she said, "I arrived at Safe Harbor yesterday from my home in Missouri. I was feeling my usual self and very excited, because I'm meeting my fiancé, Jim, at camp." Allison added, "Jim is driving to Safe Harbor from his home in Iowa. But, he called earlier today to tell me he would be delayed. He won't be arriving until tomorrow… uh, today. It's after midnight, isn't it?" Allison asked.

"Yes, it's now 1:15 in the morning. So Allison," Dr. Talbott said with a smile, "I guess it is already tomorrow."

"You know," she continued, "Jim and I met at Safe Harbor last summer. He was born and raised in Clarion. He moved to Iowa a few years ago to pursue an opportunity, but he doesn't talk about it. We've been corresponding ever since we met… kind of a long distance romance. We see each other as often as we can, our work schedules permitting. I'm just so happy, because we're getting married in Missouri in three months. We wanted to spend our one year anniversary together at Safe Harbor."

"Well, congratulations, Allison!" Dr. Talbott said with an even broader smile.

"Do you know Jim?" Allison inquired. "His name is Jim Worth."

"No, I'm sorry, Allison. I don't know Jim," he replied. Dr. Talbott continued his questioning. "Allison, before you got sick this evening, did you eat or drink anything at the camp?"

"Yes, I did. I drank bottled water from there but ate a ham and cheese sandwich I brought from home. I purchased the food at the grocery store the day before I left for Safe Harbor. I was careful to refrigerate them immediately," she proclaimed.

"Allison, how did you store the sandwich on your way here?"

"The same way I always store food when traveling, in a Styrofoam cooler filled with ice. The sandwich tasted fine. It was cold when I removed it from the cooler. I decided not to add mayonnaise just in case the ice melted prematurely," she added.

"Was that all you ate or drank up to the point of becoming ill?" Dr. Talbott questioned.

"Yes, that's all."

He went on, "Do you remember what you ate or drank twenty-four hours or so before arriving here?"

"Well, Dr. Talbott, that's easy to answer. I fasted for twenty-four hours. I try to fast one day a week. All I ever consume on those days is water and black coffee."

Dr. Talbott thanked Allison for answering his questions and performed a physical exam. He found nothing abnormal, other than signs of severe dehydration. He glanced at Marisa, who returned to the room to administer Allison's medication, and asked her to have lab come and draw Allison's blood. Dr. Talbott ordered a complete blood count, a full chemistry panel, and a stool sample for culture as well as for ova and parasites. "A stool sample?" Allison questioned with an embarrassed look.

"Yes," Dr. Talbott replied. "A stool sample can provide valuable information. It can help determine the cause of diarrhea, whether the source is bacterial, viral, or parasitic. Treatment is often based on the results of a stool culture."

"Well, if it's absolutely necessary," she said reluctantly.

"Allison, I'll be back to see you after we've obtained your test results. It will take about an hour, so try and get a little sleep while you're waiting."

"I'll try," she replied.

As he walked to the door, Dr. Talbott told Marisa he would be in Exam Room Three. He headed down the hall to evaluate the two patients just brought in by Paramedic Unit One. "Who do we have here, Derry?" Dr. Talbott asked with a big smile as he entered Exam Three.

"Well, Doctor, we have a mom and daughter from Safe Harbor, just brought in by Medic One. Mom's name is Courtney, and this is her daughter, Elizabeth. But she likes to be called Lizzy. According to the paramedics, Courtney developed a bad headache with dizziness. At about the same time, Lizzy experienced a severe coughing paroxysm, along with wheezing and shortness of breath. Lizzy improved with an albuterol treatment administered on scene by the paramedics. She now appears to be resting comfortably on low flow oxygen."

"Thanks for the report, Derry. It sounds as though these ladies are doing pretty well right now," he said, smiling at Courtney.

"By the way, Dr. Talbott, how is the patient in Exam Room Two doing?" Derry asked.

"Much better with the IV hydration," he replied.

"Doctor, please let me know if you need anything," Derry stated as she walked toward the door. Grinning at Courtney and Lizzy, Derry left the room and headed for Exam Room Six, where the Holstrom family anxiously awaited their turn for medical care.

"Hi, I'm Dr. Talbott," he said glancing at Lizzy with a pleasant smile. He loved children and had great compassion for them, along with an utmost respect for their innocence. He always made an extra effort to decrease a child's anxiety about an emergency room visit. From the patient medical records Derry had left for him, Dr. Talbott noticed Courtney was twenty-eight and Lizzie was four. "Which one of you guys is four years old?" Dr. Talbott asked jokingly with raised eyebrows.

"I am!" replied Lizzie.

"No, she is," he proclaimed, pointing to Courtney.

"No, I am!" insisted Lizzie with nervous laughter. "I am! My name is Lizzie!"

"Well, why didn't you say so, Lizzie?" Dr. Talbott asked with a wide-eyed grin.

"I did tell you!" Lizzie shouted playfully in her four-year-old voice. "He's funny, Mommy," Lizzie asserted confidently.

Dr. Talbott proceeded to shake both Courtney's and Lizzy's hands and then sat down next to Lizzy. "How are you feeling Lizzy?" he inquired.

"I feel better," she replied. "I couldn't breath before those men gave me medicine to make me feel better."

"I'm very glad to hear you're feeling better," Steve replied. "And how are you doing Courtney?" he asked with a concerned look.

"I'm so dizzy, and my head feels like it's about to explode," Courtney replied.

"Do you have a history of migraines?" Dr. Talbott asked.

"No, I rarely even get headaches. I've never experienced anything like this in my life," she responded. "The only time I've even remotely felt like this was in high school after drinking beer and smoking some pot at a friend's house," she whispered so Lizzie would not hear her.

"Courtney, do you have any chronic medical conditions or take daily medication?" he queried.

"No to both questions," she replied.

"Is it possible that Lizzie or you could have been exposed to carbon monoxide?"

"I don't think so," Courtney responded. "Doctor Talbott, could you give me something for this horrible headache?" she asked as she began rocking back and forth in pain.

"Derry, would you please come to Exam Three?" he requested over the intercom.

"Right away doctor," Derry replied from Exam Six. As Derry entered the room, Dr. Talbott requested she start an IV on Courtney. He also asked Derry to administer morphine for Courtney's headache, along with meclizine to help alleviate the dizziness.

He noticed Lizzy was frightened and looking at her mom tearfully. "Mommy will be fine, Lizzy," Steve said reassuringly as he gently wiped the tears from Lizzie's cheeks. "The medicine we're giving your mommy should make her feel better very soon."

"Okay, Doctor," Lizzy nervously replied. Steve turned on the television in the exam room and inserted a children's video into the VCR.

He then performed a physical exam on Courtney. Dr. Talbott found nothing out of the ordinary. He then focused his attention on Lizzy and, likewise, found her exam to be normal with no appreciable wheezing. Dr. Talbott ordered blood work on the two along with a CT scan of Courtney's head and an X-ray of Lizzie's chest. He wanted to see whether a hemorrhage in Courtney's brain was the cause of her severe headache and dizziness. Lizzie's chest X-ray was ordered to help determine the cause of the child's coughing episode. "Derry, I'll be in Exam Six. Please call me when the results of Courtney's head scan and Lizzie's chest X-ray return. And let me know if Courtney or Lizzie experience any further problems."

"Will do, Dr. Talbott," Derry calmly replied. Dr. Talbott then turned to Courtney, advising her he would be back to check on them. As he walked out the door, Derry asked Dr. Talbott to inform the Holstroms she would be back to attend to them as soon as possible.

"I'll be sure to let them know," he responded.

"Good evening," Steve said with a smile as he entered Exam Room Six. Picking up the ER charts, he noticed all three of the Holstroms had normal vital signs. Each, however, was experiencing severe ringing in their ears, which started earlier in the evening. He walked over to Joshua and Mary Holstrom and shook their hands. Steve asked, "Mr. and Mrs. Holstrom, were either of you or Sara ill prior to arriving at Safe Harbor?"

"No," replied Joshua, repeating the details he described to Karen McMillan and Derry. "We're all very healthy, although I do have high blood pressure and take medication for it. It's a beta-blocker. But, I've been taking it for years without any problems. Nothing has changed," said Joshua, appearing perplexed. "We arrived at camp yesterday from our home in Chicago. We were all feeling fine and very excited to be here," he added. Dr. Talbott thanked Joshua and turned to ask Mary and Sara Holstrom similar questions. Their responses were equally unremarkable.

Steve performed physical exams on each of the Holstroms and found nothing unusual. Their eardrums appeared normal. There was no abnormal fluid collection or signs of inflammation or tumor. None of the family members exhibited eye flickering, called "nystagmus," or lacked coordination when instructed to walk in a straight line, touching heel to toe. Each was able to place an index finger on the tip of his or her nose without a problem. Yet, each was experiencing profound ringing in the ears. *What's going on here?* Dr. Talbott silently mused. He asked if Joshua, Mary, or Sara had recently ingested aspirin or used oil of wintergreen liniment. Joshua responded with an unequivocal no. Joshua asked Steve the significance of his question. He responded, "Aspirin taken in excessive doses could cause ringing in the ears, which, in the medical profession, is called tinnitus. I asked about the use of oil of wintergreen because it contains an extremely large amount of methylsalicylate, a type of aspirin. If used in excess, it could conceivably cause tinnitus by being absorbed through the skin. But now," continued Dr. Talbott, "I'm simply thinking outside the box, because I can't come up with a logical explanation for why you are all experiencing such profound ringing in your ears. There are several other causes of tinnitus, but, they are typically accompanied by additional symptoms, which none of you appear to be experiencing at this time." Dr. Talbott added,

"I'd like to run some tests to check your blood sugar, electrolytes, liver and kidney function as a starting point. I would also like to order a salicylate level on each of you to determine whether aspirin may be present in your blood. I'll check on you later and let you know what the tests show as soon as the lab provides them to me." "Oh, before I forget, Derry asked me to let you know she will be back shortly to complete her nursing assessment." The family thanked Dr. Talbott as he walked out the door.

Steve walked to Exam Room Four to evaluate the family of six from Indiana sent to the ER by Shelley Markham. They had arrived while Dr. Talbott was with the Holstrom family. "Hello," said Dr. Talbott in a gentle tone as he walked into the room. "I'm Dr. Talbott, the emergency physician on duty tonight. Shelley Markham informed me you were coming. How can I be of help tonight?" Steve asked while perusing their medical charts.

"Well, Doctor," answered Coby Chambers, "while playing Ping Pong in the game room tonight at Safe Harbor, I, my wife, Ellie, and our four children suddenly developed muscle cramps. I also have this horrible headache."

"Mr. and Mrs. Chambers, when did you arrive at Safe Harbor?"

"We arrived yesterday morning from Indiana," Coby replied. "We wanted to arrive early, so we could spend the day at Clarion Lake. The weather is perfect for swimming."

"Were any of you sick prior to your arrival?" Dr. Talbott inquired.

"No sir, we were all fine," Mrs. Chambers answered.

Dr. Talbott continued, "From the time you arrived at camp, did you happen to eat or drink anything there?"

"Yes," Coby responded. "We had both lunch and supper there. The hamburgers served for lunch and the spaghetti we ate for supper tasted fine." The family members all nodded in agreement.

"And I presume," Dr. Talbott added, "all of you are healthy and not taking medication?"

"Correct," Coby replied. "We are all healthy and not on any medication."

As Steve was about to ask a follow-up question, he heard over the intercom, "Dr. Talbott. Please come to the triage area." Apologizing for the interruption, Steve excused himself and quickly left the room.

Arriving at triage, Marisa informed him the paramedics were en route from Safe Harbor with two additional patients. "What on earth is going on over there?" Steve whispered to her with obvious concern. Turning to Karen, he asked, "Please get Dr. Lisa Sommers from the Department of Infectious Disease on the phone for me. Tell her I'd like to speak with her regarding this bizarre illness we're dealing with at Safe Harbor."

"I'll page her right away doctor," Karen responded. She could sense Dr. Talbott's angst concerning this disease that had afflicted so many people at one location in such a short period of time.

Dr. Talbott returned to Exam Four to continue his evaluation of the Chambers family. "I'm very sorry for the interruption," he said apologetically. "The ER is extremely busy tonight." Steve was careful not to tell any of his patients they were all from Safe Harbor. He did not want to start a panic or unduly frighten them. "Mr. and Mrs. Chambers, I have another question. Did any of you recently consume raw pork?"

"No," replied Mrs. Chambers. "I fully cook all meat I serve to my family. I am aware of the recent E. coli outbreaks reported by the news media and familiar with trichinosis contracted by eating undercooked pork. I work in food services at one of the neighborhood schools where we live," she added. Dr. Talbott thanked Mr. and Mrs. Chambers for their thoughtful responses. He then added, "Mrs. Chambers, I apologize if I offended you, but in light of your family's symptoms, I felt it necessary to ask about food preparation."

"I understand, Doctor," she said.

After performing a physical exam on each family member, Dr. Talbott discovered nothing of significance except for the muscle spasms for which they sought treatment. He then asked Marisa to come into Exam Six. As Marisa opened the door, Dr. Talbott requested she administer weight-based doses of diazepam to each family member. He was hoping the muscle relaxant would help alleviate some of the cramping. Dr. Talbott explained, "I am ordering medication for each of you to help with the cramps. I would also like to order lab tests to see whether you are experiencing muscle breakdown for some unknown reason. Oh, and just one more question," Steve said. "Just a thought. Do any of you take medication for elevated cholesterol? Statins can sometimes cause muscle breakdown and cramping."

"No, we don't take the medication," replied Coby.

"Thank you for your answers," Steve said. "I'll be back to check on you. I'd like to see if your pain improves with the muscle relaxant. I'll also inform you of your test results as soon as they are available."

"Thank you, Dr. Talbott," Mrs. Chambers said with a smile.

As Steve entered the hallway, he heard Karen summon him. "Dr. Talbott, Dr. Sommers is on line one."

"Great. Thanks, Karen. Please transfer the call to my office." Steve did not want his patients to overhear what he was about to discuss with his colleague.

"Lisa, how are you?" he asked. "Thank you for calling back so promptly."

"Hi, Steve," she replied. "I understand you and your staff are quite busy tonight. How can I be of service?"

"Lisa, I need to ask your advice. The ER is inundated with patients from Safe Harbor. These people started coming in around midnight, and more continue to arrive as we speak. Some are walking in, while others are so sick the paramedics are transporting them. They have been arriving at the camp since yesterday morning, coming from all across the Midwest. Some are experiencing similar symptoms, while others complain of totally unrelated entities. Some have eaten the camp food and some have not. Some drank the well water at Safe Harbor, and others consumed bottled water they brought from home. Shelley Markham informed me when I spoke to her earlier the camp well was recently inspected and the water declared free from contaminants and pathogens." Dr. Talbott continued with frustration, "There seems to be no rhyme nor reason, not even a common thread as to why these people are getting sick. I've examined several of them and haven't found any useful clue or explanation as to the etiology of this mysterious illness. But, the symptoms are real and, in some cases, incapacitating." Steve went on to describe to Lisa the signs and symptoms of each patient.

"Steve, have you performed blood work and radiographic studies on these people?" Lisa inquired.

"Yes," he replied. "I'm waiting for the results, but it should not be too much longer." Just then, Karen walked into Dr. Talbott's office, handing him a computer printout of the blood test results on Allison and Courtney. She quickly left to register more patients, who continued to stream into the ER from Safe Harbor. "Lisa, I was just handed some results on two of my sicker patients. The blood tests are completely normal."

Dr. Sommers asked, "Were you able to obtain samples of the food being served at Safe Harbor and send them to the Clarion Health Department for analysis?"

"No, not yet," Steve replied. "But, when I phone Shelley Markham after we've concluded our conversation, I'll ask her to collect the samples."

"Steve, please also ask Shelley to have the health department check the camp's food storage units along with the plumbing and septic systems. Over the years," Lisa added, "I've seen some pretty sick patients due to undetected septic runoff seeping into places it shouldn't go."

"Excuse me, Dr. Talbott," Karen interrupted. She handed him the radiologist's report of Courtney's head CT and Lizzy's chest X-ray.

"Lisa, the radiology reports… they're also normal. I'm at a complete loss as to what's occurring at Safe Harbor. It's so frustrating not knowing what I'm dealing with. I've never seen anything like this in all my years of practice," he stated somberly.

"I agree, Steve, the scenario is quite perplexing. But, there has to be an explanation. Will you be admitting any of these patients to the hospital for further treatment?" Dr. Sommers inquired.

"Yes, at least three of them. I'll be admitting Allison for additional intravenous hydration and Courtney who is still experiencing a severe headache and dizziness. I'll also be keeping little Lizzy for observation. She's a sweet little four-year-old girl… and so frightened." Dr. Talbott continued with his report. "At this time, all patients appear stable and seem to be improving with treatment. Most of our walk-in patients are doing fairly well and probably stable enough to be discharged from the ER with medication. But, there are still several other patients I have yet to examine and two additional ambulances en route from Safe Harbor. The paramedics haven't yet radioed us with updated information regarding the condition of the incoming patients."

"Steve, I would be happy to participate in the care of these patients and offer my opinion. I can see them when I make hospital rounds later this morning."

"Thanks, Lisa. I am very anxious to hear what you think may be the cause of this illness along with any treatment recommendations."

"Very well, Steve. I will call you after I've had the opportunity to examine them," Lisa replied. With that, the two colleagues ended their conversation.

"Karen, would you please get Shelley Markham on the phone for me?" Dr. Talbott asked, slowly leaning back in his chair. Deep in thought, he contemplated the medical challenge facing him and his colleagues at Clarion General. After several minutes, Steve went back to check on his patients. He informed each of them their test results were normal and confessed the cause of their symptoms remained elusive. But, he assured them, with the help of the Lord, his colleagues, and further testing, the cause would eventually be revealed.

Just then, Karen announced over the intercom, "Dr. Talbott, Shelly Markham is on line two."

He walked back to his office and slowly sat down at his desk. He tiredly placed the phone to his ear. "Hello Shelley," he said with a fatigued voice. "I'm sad to report we remain perplexed as to what is going on at Safe Harbor. I've just consulted with one of my colleagues, Dr. Lisa Sommers. She is an infectious disease specialist here at the hospital. Later this morning, she plans to examine three of the sicker patients I am admitting to the hospital. At this point, neither she nor I have a good explanation as to what is making these people sick or why some are sicker than others. Shelley," Steve added, "Dr. Sommers has requested you have someone from public health check Safe Harbor's food refrigeration units along with the plumbing and septic systems to make sure they are functioning properly. She has also requested that food and water samples be collected and provided to the health department for analysis and culture."

"I will do so immediately," Shelley replied. "I'll request an inspector come out here as soon as the health department opens later this morning. Steve, will these people be okay?" she asked worriedly.

"As of now, they all appear stable. Let's see what Dr. Sommers has to offer after she's had an opportunity to examine them. I know it's easier said than done, Shelley, but please try not to worry."

"I'll try not to, but you know how much Jeremy and I love these people. They're like family to us."

"I promise to call you just as soon as I have some answers," he replied gently. "Thank you Steve. Good night."

Dr. Steve Talbott hung up the phone and once again leaned back in his chair, wondering, *So many sick people from the camp arriving from different areas of the Midwest, of differing ages, all healthy individuals yet experiencing such diverse symptoms. These people began to get sick at about the same time, no common thread and no answers as to why this is happening.* Steve took a deep breath and slowly exhaled. Closing his eyes and bowing his head in reverence, he whispered this short prayer to his Creator:

> Dear Lord, please help us find answers to the cause of this confounding illness. We need to know how to help these people who have become so ill from this strange outbreak at Safe Harbor. You have told us in Your Word that when we trust in You with all our hearts and do not lean on our own human understanding, that when we acknowledge You in all our ways, You will be faithful to direct our path. Thank you, Lord Jesus. Amen.

After spending a few moments in silence before God, Steve Talbott heard a voice that clearly spoke these words to his spirit: "Go to the camp."

CHAPTER TWO

Dr. Talbott was awakened by the loud ringing of his office telephone. Physically and emotionally drained, he had fallen asleep at his desk. Steve spent the entire night treating patients from Safe Harbor. "Hello, this is Dr. Talbott," he answered half asleep.

"Good morning Steve. This is Lisa Sommers."

"Hi Lisa. Thanks for getting back to me. What time is it?" he asked. "I must have fallen asleep at my desk."

"It's 8 AM on Saturday morning. Do you plan on sleeping the entire day, Talbott?" she asked, chuckling.

"No, just until noon," he replied sarcastically. Steve and Lisa had become good friends while in medical school and loved bantering back and forth.

"Steve, I'm calling to inform you I've just completed my examinations on Allison, Courtney, and Lizzy. Lizzy appears to be doing the best. As of now, she has no symptoms of illness. Allison, on the other hand, is still vomiting quite a bit, but her diarrhea seems to have abated. Courtney's headache persists, though not as bad as when she arrived in the ER last night. I thoroughly questioned, palpated, and prodded each of them. I reviewed their medical histories in detail. I attempted to jog their memories relative to events occurring immediately before and after arriving at Safe Harbor. After all this, I have come to a conclusion."

"And that is?" Steve quipped.

"I have concluded that I, too, am perplexed by what is occurring at that camp," she replied. "Talbott, you were quite correct when you said there appeared to be neither rhyme nor reason to the symptoms, or any clues to the cause of this outbreak. By the way," Lisa added, "has Shelley Markham managed to collect the food and water samples and has a health department official gone out to the camp yet?"

"I spoke with Shelley a few hours ago," Steve replied. "She assured me it would be taken care of this morning."

"Steve, I had another thought. Did any of your patients go swimming in Clarion Lake yesterday?"

"Yes, come to think of it," he replied. "There was a family of six who arrived from Indiana early yesterday morning so they could enjoy the day at the lake. In fact, Mr. Chambers even commented the water temperature was perfect for swimming."

"Just to be thorough, would you request someone gather samples of the lake water as well?"

"That's an excellent suggestion, Sommers! Did you come up with the idea yourself?" Steve asked, snickering.

"No, you thought of it, Steve," Lisa responded sarcastically.

"Yes, I'll ask that samples of the lake water also be taken for culture," he said.

"Lisa, a thought came to me last night while I was praying."

"What was that, Steve?"

"Can you, Shelley Markham, a Clarion Health Department official, and I meet at Safe Harbor later today? Let's take a look around the camp together to see if we can find any clues to this mystery illness."

"That sounds like a very intelligent and logical approach," Lisa replied. "Did you think of the idea, Steve?" she joked.

"No, you did, Sommers!" he responded with a laugh.

"Yes, I can meet you around 3 PM," Lisa stated seriously.

"Good," Steve replied. "I'll call Shelley and the Clarion Health Department as soon we hang up to see if that would be a convenient time for everyone."

"So, unless I hear from you," Lisa said, "we'll all plan to meet at the Safe Harbor camp office today at around three. Oh, and Steve, please don't forget to arrive awake and alert!" she said teasingly.

"Very funny, Sommers," he laughed as the two friends ended their conversation. Dr. Talbott made arrangements with Shelley

Markham and an official from the Department of Public Health for the meeting at Safe Harbor Bible Camp.

At three o'clock, Steve Talbott, Lisa Sommers, Shelley Markham, and Devin Matsen met at the camp office as planned. Devin was the health department official assigned to the investigative effort. After the team members introduced themselves, they sat down to devise a logical approach as to how they would proceed. It was agreed that Lisa and Shelley would forage in the kitchen and cafeteria. They would collect food and water samples for analysis while searching for possible sources of contamination. Devin was asked to inspect Safe Harbor's plumbing and septic system, food refrigeration units, and well casing for defects. He was also requested to drive into Clarion and obtain lake water samples. Steve would interview some of the people staying at Safe Harbor. It was his duty to try and find a common link as to the origin of the illness. At five, the foursome planned to meet back at the camp office for a progress report and an exchange of pertinent information gleaned from their individual investigations.

After collecting food and water samples, Shelley and Lisa decided to concentrate their efforts in the kitchen. They checked the food pantries for rodent droppings and even took samples from the saltshakers and pepper shakers. Lisa told Shelley about an article she once read about a man who attempted to murder his wife by placing arsenic in the family saltshaker. "How sick is that!" Shelley exclaimed. "Some people are so mentally unstable."

"Shelley, do you remember back in the mid-1970s, when some lunatic placed cyanide in acetaminophen capsules?" Lisa queried.

"Unfortunately, no one was ever caught." She pointed out, "Because what is happening here at Safe Harbor is so confusing, we have to think outside the box. This illness, with its diverse symptoms, infecting so many healthy people does not fit a specific pattern," Lisa commented. But, as a physician specializing in infectious diseases, Dr. Sommers was bound and determined to find the cause.

As the two women continued to look for clues, Devin Matsen completed his inspection of the well casing. He found nothing unusual or in disrepair. There were no cracks or leaks. The well pump was also functioning properly. He decided to take an additional well water sample for analysis, though it had been checked prior to the camp opening for summer. Devin would send this sample to the state lab for confirmatory testing. He then proceeded to inspect the camp's plumbing, septic, and refrigeration systems. Again, he detected nothing abnormal. All appeared to be operating normally and as intended. Neither a leak nor defect of any kind was discovered.

As Lisa, Shelley, and Devin were performing their tasks, Steve walked around the camp, conducting random interviews with some of the patrons. He spoke with members of the Swanson family, a clan of fifteen, who arrived the previous day from Minnesota. None of them admitted feeling ill or exhibited symptoms. Steve interviewed Andrew and Laura Bellamy, a young newlywed couple from Michigan's upper peninsula. They, too, arrived about the same time and were feeling quite normal, even after having eaten the camp food. Yet, when Dr. Talbott met with a group of four men attending the camp from a church in a town just thirty miles away, they responded quite differently. Two of the men had developed a very itchy, red rash over their bodies. The other two, however, were without symptoms. All four men ate the camp food and drank the well water. Yet, only two were symptomatic. "How can this be?" Steve muttered under his breath. He then approached three couples who drove to Safe Harbor together from Ohio. Two of the couples were married, and the third couple engaged to be married. Each pair came from a different city within Ohio. Due to strict Safe Harbor Bible Camp rules, the unmarried couple was prohibited from sleeping in the same cabin. Therefore, Steve concluded, the two were not exposed to the same cabin's environment.

Dr. Talbott learned from these conversations some people were beginning to experience symptoms of the illness, while others remained unaffected. This scenario went on for two hours. During this time, Steve failed to uncover any useful clues as to the source of this baffling disease. Perplexed and discouraged, Dr. Talbott bowed his head and asked God for His help in unmasking the cause of this outbreak. After spending a few moments in silent prayer, Steve Talbott heard in his spirit with unmistakable clarity, "Walk around the perimeter of the camp."

He was taken aback by what he had just been instructed to do. But, Steve's natural skepticism eventually gave way to careful consideration. From experience in asking the Lord for His help, Steve learned the importance of being obedient to that familiar Voice that spoke to his heart.

Safe Harbor was originally an old, thirty-acre farm purchased and renovated by Jeremy and Shelley Markham. For years, their dream was to build a family-oriented Bible camp. Its sole purpose was to preach God's Word and offer Christian families time for fellowship with God and each other. In short, it offered a time to reflect. The Markhams's dream eventually became reality, and for ten years, Safe Harbor fulfilled its intended mission by serving Christians mainly from the Midwest. The complex was designed as a group of cabins that surrounded a centrally located barn they'd converted into a chapel. Adjacent to the chapel, they'd built a modest cafeteria, where families could eat and fellowship with one another. Safe Harbor was enclosed on three sides. Small farms were situated to its north and south, while a forest abutted the camp to its west. Rural Route 30 was the access road to the east of camp, running between Safe Harbor and the town of Clarion. Several other farms could be seen on either side of Route 30, all just a short distance from the camp.

Dr. Talbott decided to initiate his search from the north and walk a clockwise path along Safe Harbor's perimeter. He would conclude his mission by the forest along the western edge of the camp. After completing his assignment, Steve would meet Lisa, Shelley, and Devin in the camp office around five as the group had agreed.

On the northern end, Steve saw nothing unusual. He noticed a small farm with its cornfield adjacent to the camp. The farmhouse appeared to be in relatively good condition but in desperate need of paint. Steve also witnessed some cows grazing in a pasture just outside the weather-beaten door of the farm's dilapidated red barn. The structure stood directly behind the farmhouse. Separating the cornfield from Safe Harbor was a length of old, rusted barbed wire. It sagged to the ground, held only by four warped wooden posts. Steve snagged one of his hiking shoes on the wire. He tripped but regained his balance without falling. Reaching the eastern boundary of the camp, he observed nothing extraordinary. In the distance, there was an old, black pickup with red stripes on its hood. As the vehicle rumbled eastward on Route 30 toward Clarion, carrying a tarp-covered load, it created a plume of brown dust. Steve noted two more farms abutting Route 30, but saw nothing that piqued his curiosity.

Arriving at Safe Harbor's southern boundary, Dr. Talbott noticed an old but well-maintained farmhouse constructed of red brick and fieldstone. The farm itself consisted of two large cornfields, a newly built barn about fifty yards behind the house, and a small wheat field adjacent to one of the cornfields. Steve remembered a conversation he overheard at the hospital several months earlier. It was regarding a middle-aged couple who recently purchased the old farmstead to get away from the "City," as Clarion residents often referred to Chicago. It was about a two-hour drive from Clarion. *The new owners did a nice job fixing up the old place*, he thought.

As he walked to the western edge of Safe Harbor, bounded by the woods, Steve found two deer carcasses lying along the tree line. This was not an unusual sight in Clarion with all its hunters. Having failed to note anything unusual, Steve realized he had less than one hundred yards left to cover. He could not understand why the Voice that so clearly instructed him to, "Walk along the perimeter of the camp," would lead him on a wild-goose chase. *Is it possible I misunderstood the instructions? Could the Voice have been my own thoughts?* he wondered. As he searched the remaining area, Steve questioned the purpose of walking the camp's perimeter. He then remembered the group was to meet back at the camp office at five. Glancing at his watch to check the time, Steve suddenly and unexpectedly found himself lying facedown on the ground. "What... in... the... world... just happened?" he shouted, grimacing from pain. Picking himself off the ground, Steve brushed leaves from his clothing. He quickly turned around to see what caused him to fall. A few feet behind him, at the wood's edge, was a large pile of leaves. Out of curiosity, he limped toward the pile to see exactly what made him trip. Plunging his hands down into the leaves, Steve felt a solid object buried deep within the pile. Just as he was about to brush away the leafy covering, Dr. Talbott heard Lisa calling to him from a distance, reminding him about their meeting. It was after five, and Steve was late. He called to Lisa, acknowledging he heard her, and began jogging toward the office.

Lisa, Shelley, Devin, and Steve each took a turn giving an account as to what they found. Devin reported the well casing, plumbing, septic system, and refrigeration units were all functioning properly. He also informed the team members he collected Clarion Lake water samples and sent them to the state lab. Devin concluded his report by stating his efforts were unsuccessful in uncovering anything substantive as to the cause of the outbreak. Next, Lisa and Shelley described how they collected various samples from the kitchen and cafeteria. They, too, were frustrated by the lack of clues. Steve went last, briefing the group as to his conversations with camp participants. He reviewed in detail what was discussed, the questions he posed to them, the different points of origin from which they came, and the various food and water sources consumed. Steve advised the group that although some camp attendees were clearly beginning to exhibit signs of the illness, others remained symptom free, even among couples.

A lengthy discussion ensued as to possible causes of the outbreak at Safe Harbor. Devin felt the illness might still be due to chemical contaminants in the food or water that had escaped detection. Dr. Sommers felt this would be unlikely due to advanced laboratory testing techniques and because of inconsistent physical findings among the patients. Shelley suggested the disease might be due to a virus that perhaps mutated, thus escaping detection. But, when asked why a mutated virus only affected people from Safe Harbor and not Clarion residents, Shelley had no explanation. Dr. Talbott brought up the possibility of terrorist activity in the area, perhaps with using undetectable chemical or biological agents. He told the group about a police memorandum he once read warning law enforcement personnel Christian and Jewish summer camps may be potential targets for terrorists. After further discussion, the group agreed none of the theories seemed plausible, considering the lack of tangible evidence.

Before the foursome adjourned, Dr. Sommers asked if there were any suggestions as to how the group should proceed with the investigation. No one had anything left to say or even suggest. They were at a loss for ideas. Lisa stared at Steve with curiosity for several seconds. Snickering at the leaves stuck to his clothing, Lisa asked why he had been rolling around in leaves instead of searching for clues. Steve responded by calmly informing Lisa he had nearly been killed by a wild animal. "It knocked me down and left me for dead!" After they all had a much-needed laugh, Steve explained that he tripped over a pile of leaves near the woods.

"A pile of leaves in late June?" queried Devin. "I've lived in several locations throughout the country. The only season I've seen piles of leaves is during autumn."

"You're right, Devin," Steve said puzzled. "I didn't think much about it being so preoccupied with finding the cause of this epidemic."

"Steve, what did you trip over?" Shelley asked with curiosity.

"I was about to brush away the leaves from this buried object when I heard Lisa ordering me to get back for our meeting. So, I jogged here without looking to see what nearly killed me," he replied laughing.

"Well then, let's go see what my esteemed colleague tripped over," Lisa suggested. "I'm curious as to what nearly killed my friend Steve Talbott," she added with an impish grin.

Arriving at the western perimeter, Shelley, Lisa, and Devin found the pile of leaves over which Steve tripped. It was located on camp property, right at the wood's edge, just as he described. Getting down on their hands and knees, they began to brush the leaves from a hard object they could all feel beneath the pile. As it became more visible, it appeared to be some sort of old wooden podium. It was rectangular, with the front and back wider than the two sides. After fully exposing the object, it measured about three feet high and two feet wide. The group noticed a unique design carved into its front panel. It was a five-pointed star with a goat's head in the center. The star, in turn, was surrounded by a completed circle. On the back of the podium, there was a carving of a man's body, on top of which was placed a goat's head. On this head, there were two horns and some sort of lighted torch between the horns. The man's right arm, holding an inverted crucifix, pointed downward. "What is this thing?" Lisa asked.

"Oh, no!" Shelley bellowed, her eyes fixed on the object. As they all turned to look at her, they could see Shelley's face had become extremely pale. Lisa asked Shelley if she felt ill. With a look of great concern, Shelley informed her friends they had just uncovered an altar for satanic worship on the premises of Safe Harbor Bible Camp. It had been buried at its very doorstep.

CHAPTER THREE

"Yes, Mrs. Morris, I am going to look into it today. We've already received several calls from other Clarion residents about it. Yes, you're describing pretty much the same thing the others... right, what they saw and heard last night. Uh huh, at the farm. I ... yes... correct. I was just about to send an officer over there to take a look. Yes, I've jotted down your phone number. Definitely. Someone will call you as soon as we have any information to report. Yes, Mrs. Morris, I'll do that. Thank you." Clarion Police Chief Larry Doyle stared at the receiver before slamming it down onto its cradle. He sat at his desk for a few seconds, shaking his head in frustration. Getting up from his chair, the chief walked out of his office. As he entered the briefing room, he saw Sergeant Roger Fleming seated at one of the computers, completing his shift report. "Sergeant Fleming, I want to talk to you." Fleming knew his boss, Chief Doyle, was a respected, no-nonsense cop. He rose to the position of chief of police from the ranks, having been a member of the Clarion Police Department for thirty-five years. Roger, along with his fellow officers, learned from experience not to upset the chief.

"Yes sir," Fleming replied as Chief Doyle approached him.

"Roger, I want you to drive out to the Clayworth place. Take a look around for anything suspicious and report back to me."

"What's the problem, sir?" Roger inquired.

"This phone has been ringing off the hook since last night. I just got off the phone with Amanda Morris. She and who knows how many other Clarion residents are upset about some strange lights, weird sounds—who in the heck knows what they're talking about—coming from the Clayworth residence last night."

"Who are the Clayworths, Chief?"

"You know," the chief responded gruffly, "they're the couple who moved to Clarion from the City a few months ago. They bought the old Rayburn farm. You know, the farm with the red brick and fieldstone house off Route 30 near Safe Harbor."

"Oh, yeah," Fleming said, recalling the property, "I know the place. The Rayburns were a nice old couple. They were married for close to fifty years and real active in their church. I think they were involved in some sort of missionary work." Fleming continued, "It's a shame they both died so unexpectedly. By the way, Chief, did the medical examiner ever find the cause of death?"

"No," the chief responded. "The examiner concluded the Rayburns died of natural causes. He initially thought the two may have died as the result of carbon monoxide poisoning from a faulty furnace. But no carbon monoxide was ever detected in the postmortem blood samples." Doyle glanced down as he tried to remember specifics of the case. "The Clayworths bought the Rayburn property and moved in before Mr. and Mrs. Rayburn had time to turn cold in their graves." Looking up at Roger, the chief said, "Take a squad car and drive out there. Talk to the Clayworths, inquire as to their activities last night, and request permission to look around. Report to me as soon as you can, so I have something to tell the 'overly concerned' citizens of Clarion."

"Will do, Chief," the sergeant replied. "I'll let you know what I find." Roger immediately jumped into his police cruiser and drove out to the old Rayburn farm.

Steve and Lisa headed directly to the hospital after their trip to Safe Harbor. They were anxious to see how their patients were faring. Dr. Talbott made a quick visit to the ER, giving the staff a heads up they would be receiving more sick people from the camp. He and Lisa took the elevator to the fourth floor, where the infectious disease isolation unit was located. Allison, Courtney, and Lizzie were assigned negative pressure rooms on the unit until it was determined their disease was not spread by airborne route. As the two physicians entered Allison's room, they saw Derry White at the foot of Allison's bed. "Hello ladies," Dr. Talbott said with his usual smile. "Derry, I see you came up here to visit Allison."

"Oh hello," Derry replied, somewhat startled. "Yes, I thought I'd take a short break from my ER duties to see how Allison is doing."

"Very thoughtful of you, Derry. But," he continued, "didn't Marisa take care of Allison last night in the ER?"

"Yes," Derry answered nervously, "but Marisa and I always help each other with patients when the ER gets busy." Derry smiled at Allison and said, "I should get back down to the ER. I've exceeded my break time. But, I promise to come back and visit with you very soon."

"Thank you for looking in on me Derry," Allison moaned.

Allison appeared very weak, barely able to prop herself up in bed. "Allison," said Dr. Sommers, "you were feeling so much better yesterday when I came to see you. What happened?"

"Well, Dr. Sommers," she replied, "I was doing much better. But, just a little while ago, I got sick again. I became very nauseated and started to vomit."

Dr. Sommers responded, "I'm going to prescribe another medication that should help you. I will check on you tomorrow morning." Allison sat up briefly to thank Steve and Lisa for coming to see her and then her head flopped back down onto the pillow.

Leaving Allison's room, the two walked down the corridor to visit Courtney and Lizzie. As they entered the room, Steve and Lisa observed Courtney, grimacing in pain as she held her head. They also noticed Lizzie sleeping soundly and in no distress. "What's wrong, Courtney?" Lisa whispered.

"Oh, I'm not feeling very good," she responded. "This horrible headache came back about a half hour ago, even worse than last night. I'm so dizzy and lightheaded."

"Courtney, I want to prescribe an additional medication for you," Dr. Sommers said. She immediately left the room, walking to the nurse's station to write the order.

Dr. Talbott remained in the room to pose additional questions. "Courtney, when did the headache return and get this bad? I thought you had improved?"

"I did feel much better, Dr. Talbott," she reported. "But the headache came back with a vengeance about twenty minutes ago." He then inquired how Lizzie was doing, looking at her as she slept. "She's doing well," Courtney said. "Lizzie started to wheeze again a while ago. But, she's so sweet. I listened to her pray, 'God, please take my sickness away, and make Mommy better, too.' Soon afterward, Lizzie just fell asleep."

"Oh, that we could all possess childlike faith," Steve remarked.

"Doctor Talbott," Courtney said. "I would like to thank you and Dr. Sommers for all your kindness. And please give Marisa our thanks for coming up here to visit us."

"Marisa came to see you today? Steve queried.

"Yes," Courtney replied. "She came to see us just before Lizzie and I got sick again."

"Well," Steve said, "I'll be sure to thank Marisa for you when I see her. Feel better, Courtney, and please give Lizzie a big hug from me when she awakes from her nap!"

As Dr. Talbott left the room, he headed to the nurse's station to chat with Dr. Sommers. "Lisa, what does your intuition tell you? What do you think is going on?"

"Steve, I simply don't know yet. I've just written the order for Courtney's new pain medication." He then told Lisa what Courtney described regarding Lizzie's prayer… how Lizzie stopped wheezing and fell asleep. "Steve, please don't bring up that religious stuff. You know how I feel about it! I refuse to believe in a God who allows so much evil to befall humankind." Steve reluctantly agreed to refrain from broaching the subject, at least for the time being. He understood the great emotional pain Lisa suffered as a child because of the loss of both her parents in a fiery car crash. Steve suggested he and Lisa go to the hospital cafeteria for a cup of coffee. There, they could discuss the medical dilemma plaguing the Bible camp and attempt to come up with a diagnosis and treatment plan.

Home at the parsonage from Safe Harbor, Shelley Markham sat down on the sofa beside her husband, Pastor Jeremy Markham. She informed him of the altar the group had uncovered. "Jeremy, we found it buried on the west side of camp by the woods. I cannot… I will not ignore this!" she angrily declared. "Who shall we notify to dispose of it?"

"Shelley, I'm still trying to come to grips with the fact you found a satanic altar on camp property. Why would anyone want to place such a thing there? And for what purpose?" he asked with a concerned look. "Hon, this disturbs me, too," Jeremy added. "Why don't we contact Larry Doyle and ask his advice?"

"Excellent idea," she replied. "I'll phone him right now." After the first ring, a male voice answered, "Clarion Police Department. How can we assist you?" "Hello, this is Shelley Markham. May I please speak to Chief Doyle?"

"Please hold," the voice responded. "I'll try and locate him."

After a brief pause, Shelley heard, "Hello, Chief Doyle speaking. How can I be of service?"

"Hello Larry. This is Shelley Markham."

"Oh, hi Mrs. Markham. I do apologize. I had intended to call you to explain why I wasn't able to make it last week. You know, job-related absence. But, I promise to be there tomorrow." Larry Doyle had recently begun attending Pastor Markham's church and had volunteered to sing in the choir as a baritone.

"Chief, I wish this were related to your church attendance," Shelley replied. "Unfortunately, the nature of my call is related to law enforcement."

"How then may I be of help, Mrs. Markham?"

"Larry, did you read this morning's edition of the *Clarion Herald*, regarding Safe Harbor?" she inquired.

"Yes, I did," he replied. "The entire town is talking about it. All those people getting so sick."

Shelley continued, "Steve Talbott, Lisa Sommers, Devin Matsen from the health department, and I spent several hours at the camp earlier today. We did some investigating on our own."

"What were you looking for?" Chief Doyle questioned with a serious tone of voice.

"We obtained food and water samples, walked around looking for any sort of clue, and spoke with some of the people in attendance, hoping to find answers. But," Shelley continued, "while Steve Talbott was walking along the western edge of the camp property by the woods, he stumbled over an object concealed beneath a pile of leaves. Larry, it turned out to be a satanic altar buried right on Safe Harbor property. I'm absolutely livid that someone would do such a thing!"

"Mrs. Markham, would you be able to identify this object if you saw it again?" Doyle questioned.

"Yes, we would all be able to identify that hideous thing!" she exclaimed.

"Is it still there? Has anyone moved it?" Doyle anxiously inquired.

"It's still there under the leaves," Shelley responded.

"Good. Just keep it there," the chief ordered. "I've just dispatched Sergeant Fleming to the Clayburn residence regarding a separate matter. Their place isn't far from the woods where you found the altar." Doyle added, "I'll have Fleming run over there to take a look."

"Oh, the old Rayburn farm just to the south of Safe Harbor?" Shelley asked.

"That's right," the chief replied matter-of-factly. "But, Mrs. Markham, I'm not sure what I can do about the altar. To my knowledge, no law has been broken."

"Chief Doyle, I would be grateful for anything you can do about moving that wretched thing from the camp."

"I'll do what I can, Mrs. Markham. See you in church tomorrow morning for Sunday worship. Good-bye."

After they hung up, Chief Doyle made a quick phone call before returning to his duties. Shelley sat back down beside her husband, continuing her narrative of all the actions taken by the group. As Pastor Jeremy listened intently to his wife's detailed account, she unwittingly provided him with an important topic for a future sermon.

Arriving at the Clayworth residence, Sergeant Fleming stepped out of his vehicle and approached the front door of the farmhouse. After several knocks, the door slowly opened and a man appeared. He was of average height, in his mid-fifties, and dressed in clothes worn by "hippies" during the sixties. Fleming also noticed the man had black, shoulder-length hair with gray streaks. A well-groomed mustache joined a tuft of long hairs on the individual's chin, completely encircling his mouth. "What can I do for you officer?" the man asked.

"Sir, I'm Sergeant Roger Fleming from the Clarion Police Department. Are you the owner of this property?"

"Yes sir, I am. My name is James Clayworth."

"Mr. Clayworth, I'm here to investigate several complaints we have received from concerned Clarion residents. They reported seeing strange lights and hearing some unusual sounds coming from your property last night."

"Oh, is *that* why you're here?" Clayworth asked with a look of relief. "I can explain all that very easily. My wife and I just acquired this property a few months ago. We often talked about buying a farm in this location for years. We couldn't wait to leave the city and relocate to pursue the serenity of country living. We held a party here last night in celebration of our new purchase."

"Sir," Sergeant Fleming asked, "can you explain the strange lights and sounds the people in town were describing?"

"Strange lights and sounds?" Clayworth asked, appearing confused. "Oh, the torches!" he finally responded. "Yes, I can explain. For the party, we lit torches all around the house. We also built a fairly large bonfire in the pit over there," he explained, pointing toward the barn behind the house. "The wind last night must have caused the flames to flicker back and forth. As for the strange noises, we were listening to our new age CDs. The sound system was cranked up pretty loudly. I suppose," Clayworth added, "it could have sounded like weird noises to people who dont have an appreciation for our type of music."

"Sir, would you mind if I take a look around to confirm what you have just told me?" Roger asked.

"Sure, feel free to have a look-see and take your time," Clayworth answered. "I have nothing to hide. I'll be inside the house if you have any questions." Sergeant Fleming thanked Clayworth and began searching the premises. As he circled the house, Roger saw at least fifty torches, standing upright in the ground, surrounding the property. The scent of burned kerosene suggested their recent use. Roger headed to the barn directly behind the home. Between the two edifices, Fleming observed the fire pit Clayworth had mentioned. It was encircled by several large rocks. The pit contained a considerable amount of smoldering ashes. The sergeant could smell the aroma of recently burned firewood, along with an offensive odor he could not readily identify. Entering the barn, Roger recognized the usual farm implements lining the walls and hanging from its rafters. Hay covered the floor of the barn, but there were no animals present. Continuing his search, Fleming noticed what appeared to be several pieces of furniture. They were neatly stacked against a wall and covered with a large tarp. A black pickup was parked against an adjacent wall. An object of similar shape and size to the ones stacked against the wall had been placed on its side in the truck bed. It, too, was covered with a heavy tarp. Everything appeared to be in order.

As he was completing the search, Roger's radio sounded. It was Chief Doyle, requesting that Fleming go to the location of the altar Shelley described. When he arrived at the site, Roger was to call the chief. As Fleming started walking back to the front door of the house, he saw Mr. Clayworth staring at him through one of the windows. As their eyes met, Clayworth quickly closed the curtains. Roger knocked on the front door. When Clayworth appeared, Fleming thanked him for his cooperation. As Roger turned to leave, he noticed how close in proximity the Clayworth residence was to Safe Harbor. The camp appeared to be only two hundred yards away. Both Safe Harbor and the woods to its west could be clearly seen from the front of the farmhouse. So close to the altar site, Sergeant Fleming figured he would walk.

As he crossed the western perimeter of the camp toward the woods, Fleming noted the two deer carcasses seen earlier by Steve Talbott. Approaching the dead deer, Roger observed large incisions that extended the length of each carcass belly. The incisions were held together by rope, much like a surgeon closes a wound with suture. Sergeant Fleming decided to cut the rope with his pocketknife to see why the deer bellies had been incised. Removing one of the ties, Roger leaped back reflexively, as two dead dogs tumbled from within the deer's belly. Stunned, he slowly removed the rope from the second deer carcass. Another dead canine rolled out of the gutted belly. "What in h is this?" he shouted angrily. Enraged because of his fondness for dogs, he quickly scanned the area, hoping to find the culprit who committed this heinous act. "I can't believe people having such disregard for animals are allowed to live!" he fumed.

Regaining his composure, Fleming continued to walk along the edge of the woods adjoining Safe Harbor in his quest to find the mysterious altar. Eventually locating the pile of leaves, Roger discovered only a hole in the ground. He saw no wooden altar anywhere in or near the vicinity. As the chief had instructed, Roger radioed his boss to apprise him of the situation. He informed Chief Doyle only an empty hole remained where the altar was reported to have been buried. The chief ordered Roger to return to the Clayworth residence and wait for him there. Doyle wanted to meet Fleming so they could look around together.

Arriving at the Clayworth property, Chief Doyle parked his unmarked squad car next to Roger's cruiser. Doyle told Fleming he wanted to initiate their search at the altar site. Leading the way, Roger trudged with the chief along the same route he had just taken. Perusing the area, Doyle was quick to notice a set of partially concealed tire tracks directly behind the altar site. The tracks appeared to wind through the woods in the direction of the Clayworth farm. Pointing to the trail, Doyle questioned Roger as to why he neglected to report the finding. Sergeant Fleming admitted he failed to notice them, having been distracted by his discovery of the dead canines. Chief Doyle admitted that he, too, had a passion for dogs. But, he cautioned Fleming not to allow his emotions to interfere with a police investigation. After Roger apologized for overlooking this piece of evidence, the chief told him to look at the tracks. "These ruts were likely made by truck tires due to their width. And do you notice their depth? It looks as though the vehicle may have been hauling a load." Roger sheepishly nodded, embarrassed by his failure to notice them.

The two then walked to where the deer carcasses lay, looking for clues along the route. Gazing at the three dead canines that had been stuffed into the gutted deer, Chief Doyle recalled a statewide police memo he recently received. He told Roger the memo described how certain satanic cults would perform animal sacrifices during their "religious" rituals. The cultists understood bones remained after burning the sacrificed animals. The bones could then be used as evidence against the cult and its activities. So, the satanists would kill a deer, eviscerate it, and place the dead sacrificial animals into the deer's abdominal cavity. The deer carcass would then be moved to the side of a road, where personnel from the Department of Natural Resources would unwittingly dispose of it. *How deceptively clever*, Roger thought. "I'd love to catch them in the act," he snarled, tapping on the handgrip of his Taser.

"Fleming, let's follow these tire tracks to see where they lead." Nodding, Roger and the chief trekked through the woods along the ruts. The tracks eventually led to the back door of the Clayworth barn. "I'm going to pay Mr. Clayworth a visit," Doyle declared. Rapping on the front door, the chief introduced himself to Clayworth. Doyle then requested permission for a second search of the property. After Clayworth reluctantly agreed, Chief Doyle and his sergeant immediately walked toward the back of the house. As the two approached the fire pit, Doyle suddenly stopped. Staring into the pit, the chief pointed to several charred bones. "Did you happen to see these, Roger?" Disturbed by the sight, Fleming admitted he failed to notice them but now recognized the odor he had been unable to identify. It was burned dog flesh. "This is the reason cultists stuff their sacrificial animals into gutted deer," the chief quipped. "Bones don't burn very well." Entering the barn, Doyle and Fleming removed the tarp from the pieces of furniture Roger reported having seen. The pieces appeared to be handmade wood carvings, all rectangular and standing approximately three feet tall. They appeared to be only partially completed. There were no markings on the pieces, and nothing seemed suspicious to Doyle.

The men walked over to the black pickup, still parked against the adjacent wall. Chief Doyle noticed the vehicle was equipped with oversized tires. He also observed several red stripes on the truck's hood, taking the shape of a five-pointed star. There was nothing within the bed of the truck. "Chief, when I came in here earlier, there was definitely something covered with a tarp in the back of this truck," Roger said.

"Sergeant Fleming, let's have a talk with Mr. Clayworth," Doyle stated with conviction. As Clayworth opened the door, Chief Doyle was quick to notice a pair of binoculars on a table beneath one of the living room windows that faced Safe Harbor and the woods. "Mr. Clayworth, would you mind if I asked you a few questions?" Doyle requested.

"Ask away," Clayworth responded curtly.

"Have you recently driven your black pickup that's parked in the barn?"

"No sir," Clayworth stated. "Besides, it's not my pickup. It's my wife's truck."

Doyle continued, "Mr. Clayworth, did your wife place anything heavy into the back of her truck or drive it over to those woods recently?" The chief pointed to the area where he discovered the tire tracks.

"I haven't noticed anything in the back of her truck lately, and to my knowledge, she has no reason to drive into the woods," Clayworth responded. "But," he added, "my wife does drive the truck into Clarion when she buys groceries or does errands."

"Sir, who does all that nice woodworking against the wall in the barn?" Doyle queried.

"I do," Clayworth answered, smiling. "It's been a hobby of mine for years."

"Did you or Mrs. Clayworth move any of them from your barn recently?" asked Doyle.

"No, not recently," Clayworth responded. "But I do move a piece from time to time when someone wants to purchase one of them."

"And you didn't haul any recently," the chief asked a second time.

"No, I have not."

"Mr. Clayworth, have any animals or family pets recently disappeared from your property?" the chief queried, thinking about the bones in the fire pit.

"No, my wife and I don't raise animals or own any pets," Clayworth said.

"Well, thanks for your time, Mr. Clayworth. I'm sorry to have bothered you, but it's our job to investigate all complaints registered with the police department."

"Not a problem," replied Clayworth.

As Chief Doyle and Sergeant Fleming walked toward their vehicles, Doyle turned toward Roger. He whispered to Fleming, "I want to talk to you as soon as we get back into town." The two left the Clayworth property and headed back to Clarion. As he drove, Chief Doyle phoned Shelley Markham. He informed her the altar was missing and had been moved from the site. Only a hole remained where it had been buried. Troubled by the news, Shelley thanked Chief Doyle for his help. She immediately contacted Steve Talbott to inform him of the situation. Baffled by the disappearance of the altar, Steve and Shelley agreed to pray and seek the Lord's counsel. The two then planned to discuss the next steps that should be taken and what the Lord might reveal to them while praying individually.

Shortly after they hung up, Steve's cell phone rang. It was Lisa Sommers, calling with even more disturbing news. Lisa informed him she had received a phone call requesting her immediate return to the hospital. The nursing staff informed her Allison and Courtney had taken, "a sudden turn for the worse." Lisa advised Steve that she observed Allison vomiting uncontrollably and that the diarrhea returned, now bloody. Allison's blood pressure dropped to a dangerously low 65/50, and she was barely conscious. Dr. Sommers also reported Allison was so severely dehydrated, her urinary output was negligible, and she was now in acute renal failure. Allison was so critically ill, Dr. Sommers ordered her immediately transferred to the Intensive Care Unit. Lisa even expressed concern Allison might not survive this new insult to her body.

Dr. Sommers next discussed with Steve how Courtney's condition also began to rapidly deteriorate. While examining Courtney, Lisa witnessed her fever spike to over 104 degrees. Courtney's headache was so severe she began vomiting and developed blurred vision. Dr. Sommers feared Courtney might have contracted bacterial meningitis, a true medical emergency. She ordered Courtney moved to the intensive care unit, where Courtney would be given high doses of antibiotics and prepared for an emergency spinal tap.

If that news had not been bad enough, Lisa reported several other patients he had initially seen in the ER returned to the hospital in critical condition. Joshua Holstrom, who had been complaining of ringing in his ears the night before, returned by ambulance with signs of a stroke. Joshua's wife and daughter, fortunately, had not gotten any worse. Mrs. Chambers, who had been experiencing diffuse muscle aches, returned by ambulance with a heart attack. More and more people from Safe Harbor continued to pour into the ER with various complaints, some requiring hospitalization. Steve audibly distraught, thanked Lisa for the update. Steve advised Lisa he would immediately return to Clarion General and meet her in the ICU. Their conversation having ended, he got down onto his knees and prayed to his Heavenly Father:

> Father, You know all things. Nothing is by any means hidden from You. Lord, I ask that You would open, not only our physical senses, but also our spiritual eyes, ears, minds, and hearts so we can understand the nature of this debilitating disease that remains so elusive to us. Help us, Lord, to discover the cause of this illness afflicting so many of the people at Safe Harbor and the means by which to help them. We know from Your Word that You are Jehovah Rophe, the God Who heals us from all our afflictions, and that by Jesus' stripes we are healed.[1] We also have confidence You are able to do exceedingly abundantly above all that we ask or think.[2] I thank you, Father, for Your everlasting mercy and loving kindness toward us. You alone, Lord, are our refuge and strength, a very present help in times of trouble.[3] We, therefore, have no reason to fear. Thank you, Father, in Jesus' precious name I pray. Amen.

1 Is. 53:5
2 Eph. 3:20
3 Ps. 46:1

After making his heartfelt petition to the Lord, Steve got into his car and left for the hospital. As he drove, the following verse of Scripture seemed to leap into his mind, speaking these words to his spirit:

My people are destroyed for lack of knowledge.[1]

---

1 Hos.4:6

CHAPTER FOUR

As Dr. Talbott opened the door to the brightly illuminated eight-bed ICU, he observed a flurry of activity. IV pumps beeped as they delivered pre-measured doses of life-saving medications to critically ill patients. Mechanical ventilators hummed while forcing essential oxygen into the lungs of those patients requiring life support. Multicolor monitors displayed each patient's heart rhythm on a console located in the center of the large, arena-shaped room. Each of the four ICU nurses on duty was assigned two patients. These specialized caregivers were accustomed to the rapid pace inherent to the intensive care setting. Steve admired how quickly yet carefully they administered the prescribed treatments to their patients. Simultaneously, nurse's aides prepared beds for additional patients being transferred to ICU from the ER. Steve could hear Dr. Sommers shout sequential orders to the nurses: "Get a second IV line started in Courtney's arm. Give her the antibiotics as soon as possible. Please set up an LP tray stat, so I can perform a spinal tap on her to rule out meningitis.

"Dr. Sommers, at what rate do you want Allison's IV fluids running?" asked Heidi, one of the nurses." "Heidi, Allison is severely dehydrated and has developed acute renal failure." So, please give her an initial 500ml bolus of saline. Then, run the saline drip at 125ml per hour," Lisa shouted, appearing somewhat harried. She added, "We have to rehydrate Allison but slowly, or we could cause her to go into congestive heart failure." "Who's the intensive care MD on duty now?" Dr. Sommers queried.

"It's Dr. Martin. He's helping the cardiologist with three new patients just admitted to the cardiac care unit from the ER. All three are experiencing chest pain. One patient is having a full-blown heart attack. The ER also just called us with a patient update. They're transferring two patients to ICU, one with an acute stroke and the other with severe shortness of breath due to a large pulmonary embolus (blood clot in the lung). We informed Dr. Martin they are being transferred up here within the next ten minutes. He told us he would return as soon as possible." Heidi then informed Dr. Sommers all of the ICU beds were now occupied. "The ICU is at full capacity, and we are unable to accommodate any more patients."

Good Lord, what are we going to do? Lisa thought. *The ER staff is scrambling to care for the influx of patients from Safe Harbor. We may have to transfer some patients to another hospital if they require an ICU setting. Lord, what is going on at that camp?* Lisa mused. "And *why* do I keep saying 'Lord'?" she muttered sarcastically. "Since when does He help in times of crisis? My parents were very kind and generous people. Why didn't God allow them to survive that horrible car crash? And why would a loving God have ever allowed it to happen?" she questioned. Lisa seethed with anger toward God for taking her parents from her while she was such a young child.

"Lisa, what is going on in here?" Steve shouted as he entered the controlled chaos. "I stopped in the ER before coming up here. It's like a disaster scene down there with all the patients coming in from Safe Harbor. And it doesn't appear to be much better here in ICU. We just had coffee together in the cafeteria, and everything seemed status quo. What happened? And what has happened to Allison and Courtney? They were stable when we looked in on them a couple of hours ago."

"Steve, I've ordered more IV saline for Allison. She has lost so much bodily fluid from all the vomiting and diarrhea, she's gone into renal failure.. Courtney spiked a temp of 104.2, and I'm concerned she may have bacterial meningitis. I have prescribed high doses of ceftriaxone and vancomycin,[1] given her a bolus of methylprednisolone,[2] and asked the nurses to prepare her for an LP."[3] Dr. Sommers continued, "Three patients with chest pain were just admitted to CCU. One of them is Mrs. Chambers, who is actively infarcting."[4] The ER is preparing to transfer to ICU both Mr. Holstrom with a stroke and another patient with a pulmonary embolus. All five patients are from Safe Harbor."

Dumbfounded and at a loss for words, Dr. Talbott immediately went to see Allison. He stood at her bedside, watching as Allison's heartbeat danced across the cardiac monitor in a rapid rhythm from severe dehydration. Two IVs were delivering much-needed fluids to help replenish her depleted intravascular volume. A nasal cannula had also been placed into Allison's nostrils to provide her dehydrated body with essential oxygen. "Allison, how are you feeling?" Steve

---

1 Ceftriaxone and Vancomycin are both potent intravenous antibiotics.
2 Methylprednisolone is a potent intravenous steroid to help to prevent brain swelling in a patient with meningitis.
3 Spinal tap, or LP, involves inserting a needle into an area of the lower back to extract cerebrospinal fluid for analysis.
4 Medical terminology for heart attack.

asked softly. All Allison could do in response was to move her head slowly from side to side. "You'll feel better in no time with the IV fluids. Don't lose heart," he said trying to encourage her. *Dear God, what's happened to her?* Steve silently asked his Creator. He gently touched Allison's shoulder and then left her room.

Lisa met Steve as he exited, noticing the tears welling up in his eyes. "Steve, you know we're doing all we can for her," Lisa whispered while gently squeezing his hand.

"I'd like to look in on Courtney. How is she doing? Is she as sick as Allison?" he queried.

"I'm afraid Courtney is extremely ill, too," Lisa replied. "I'll have a better idea after we've obtained results from the spinal tap I'm about to perform."

The two doctors walked into Courtney's room, located at the opposite end of the ICU from Allison's. Dr. Talbott picked up Courtney's chart and saw her fever had continued to rise. It was now approaching 105 degrees. Courtney was perspiring profusely. An IV had been placed into each of her arms to hydrate her and to deliver essential medication. "Courtney, how are you feeling?" Steve asked.

"Dr. Talbott, I've never felt so terrible in my life. This is the worst headache I've ever experienced. I'm so cold. I can't stop shivering."

"It's due to the high fever," he stated. "The antibiotics you're receiving should start to work soon."

"Courtney, I'm about to give you medication through your IV that will make you feel drowsy," said Dr. Sommers. "I'm also going to inject a small area of your lower back with an anesthetic so you won't feel pain from the spinal tap needle."

"Okay, Dr. Sommers. Please, let's get this over with," Courtney whispered in a voice weakened by her illness.

"This will not take long," Lisa told her patient reassuringly.

After completing the procedure, Dr. Sommers placed the four test tubes filled with Courtney's cerebrospinal fluid into a container. She held the tubes up to the light, showing them to Steve. Lisa was shocked at how clear the fluid appeared. "Bacterial meningitis typically causes the cerebrospinal fluid to become somewhat cloudy. The clarity of Courtney's CSF suggests a different diagnosis," Lisa said. "Steve, I'm simply baffled. I would have wagered money Courtney had bacterial meningitis. We'll have to wait for the final culture results to make a definitive diagnosis."

"Lisa, I'm going to the lab," Steve said. "I want to obtain a preliminary report regarding Allison's stool culture. We collected the sample the other night in the ER. With all Allison's vomiting and diarrhea, her stool culture should be positive for some type of infection." Dr. Talbott quickly left the ICU and headed down to the lab, located on the first floor of the hospital next to the ER. Walking past the emergency room waiting area, he saw it overflowing with patients, waiting to be treated by the beleaguered ER staff. As Dr. Talbott entered the lab, he asked a technician for Allison's preliminary culture report. He was amazed when he saw it was absolutely normal after twenty-four hours. "I can't believe it," he quietly muttered. *The forty-eight-hour test result will tell us conclusively whether the etiology of Allison's illness is infectious,* he thought. Steve phoned the ICU and updated Lisa with Allison's preliminary results. After they conferred, both physicians agreed whatever was causing the people from Safe Harbor to become so ill, particularly Allison and Courtney, remained an enigma. Now six o'clock on Saturday night, Lisa and Steve both admitted they were beginning to experience fatigue from the long and stressful day. Dr. Sommers, however, decided to remain in ICU a little longer to observe her ill patients.

Emotionally drained, Steve carefully considered the possible causes of this medical challenge. He thought back to what the Voice had said to him: "My people are destroyed for lack of knowledge." *What is He trying to tell me?* Steve wondered. *Destroyed for lack of WHAT knowledge?* "Lord, what are You trying to tell me?" he whispered with angst. Just then he realized he needed spiritual guidance in this matter. "I'm going to phone Pastor Markham for advice."

After two rings, Shelley picked up the telephone. "Hello, Markham residence."

"Hi Shelley, this is Steve Talbott."

"Oh, hello Steve. What can I do for you?"

"Shelley, I'm sorry to be calling on a Saturday night, but I have to talk to your husband regarding something of importance. Is Pastor Jeremy available?"

"Yes, he's in his study working on tomorrow's sermon. I'll go get him for you."

"Hi, good evening, Steve," Pastor Markham answered.

"Pastor Jeremy, I won't keep you long, but I must ask you a question regarding the Safe Harbor outbreak."

"Please ask," the pastor responded.

"I'm sure Shelley informed you how very ill many of these people have become."

"Yes, she's told me," Jeremy replied.

Steve continued, "As I was praying last night, I believe the Lord spoke to my heart. I believe He spoke these words to me: 'My people are destroyed for lack of knowledge.' It is unclear to me as to what these words mean. What is God trying to tell me? And, could it possibly be related to what is happening to our patients from Safe Harbor?"

After a brief moment of silence, Pastor Markham replied. "Steve, the Lord has been speaking to my heart as well regarding this urgent matter. I, too, have been praying and fasting about the events unfolding at Safe Harbor. I truly believe the Lord has impressed upon my spirit these dear people are not getting sick from natural causes."

"What do you mean?" Steve queried.

Pastor Markham continued, "The Lord touched my heart earlier today, while Shelley described to me all that you and your team uncovered at Safe Harbor. I believe the Lord spoke these verses to my spirit: 'Everyone did what was right in his own eyes,[1]' and, 'There is a way which seems right to a man, but its end is the way of death.'"[2]

"Pastor Jeremy, what relevance do these Bible passages have to what is happening at Safe Harbor?" Steve asked incredulously.

"Tell me, Steve, have you ordered tests on these people?"

"Yes, we have," Steve responded.

"And what have the tests revealed?" the pastor asked.

"So far, all patient test results have been normal," Steve replied.

"And have the prescribed treatments been effective in improving the condition of your patients?" the pastor asked.

"No, they have not" Steve replied. "Conventional treatments do not seem to be working. And it has been very baffling to us physicians at the hospital," Dr. Talbott added.

"Steve, I truly believe the Lord is telling us we must look to another cause of this illness, perhaps a supernatural one."

"Pastor Jeremy, are you trying to tell me, in this day and age, *witchcraft* is the cause of this outbreak? Are you serious? And even if someone were to believe in the power of witchcraft, how could it wreak such havoc over professed Christians attending a Christian camp?"

1 Judges 17:6.
2 Proverbs 14:12.

"Steve, I've seen its power while on missions trips to third world countries. But, I believe it's more than just witchcraft, voodoo, or a perverse spirit of divination at work here. In order for these evil entities to impact a person's life negatively, a door would have to be opened by that person to allow entrance. In fact, I believe so strongly this is the case, I have changed the theme of my sermon for tomorrow morning. Will you be in church, Steve? I would like very much for you to attend. I want you to consider what I have to say and what God's Word tells us about the subject."

"Yes, I definitely plan to attend," Steve replied. "Well, Pastor, I must get back to work. Thank you for your time, and I'll see you in church tomorrow." With a good-bye from Pastor Jeremy, the conversation ended. Overwhelmed by what he just heard, Dr. Talbott decided to go to the hospital library and retrieve information on witchcraft, wicca, and satanism. He had doubts about how harmless little incantations, spells, charms, or rituals could cause humans to become ill, especially praying Christians.

How very bizarre. Has my good friend Jeremy Markham become delusional and gone off the deep end? Steve wondered as he sat down in front of the computer to research the topic. Typing "witchcraft" and "satanism" into the search engine, he could hardly believe all the Websites that referenced the subject. As Dr. Talbott explored the different sites, he came across such things as "wiccan magic spells," "charms," and "incantations." He even clicked onto a Website that actually described how to conjure up evil spirits. Steve perused information discussing the eight wiccan "sabbats," or celebrations, where candles of various colors surrounded the altars. Often employed during these ceremonies were pagan foods, plants, herbs, and gemstones, along with pictures of mythical creatures such as fairies, dragons, and satyrs (part goat and part human). Steve sat up in his chair and took notice when he read one of the eight sabbats, "Litha," was considered by wiccans to be one of the best times of the year to cast spells and perform powerful magic. What made the hair stand up on the back of Steve's neck was when he read Litha is typically celebrated on June 21, the summer solstice. "Good Lord," he said loudly. "The outbreak at Safe Harbor began on Friday night, June 21!" *Could there be some truth to what Jeremy said?* Steve wondered. Continuing to research the topic, Dr. Talbott learned there were some differences between wiccan and satanic practices. However, both were based on the philosophy of a follower living life his way rather than God's way as written in the pages of Scripture. Steve learned both wiccans and satanists utilized witchcraft in certain ceremonies. He thought back to his college days, where he met a self-proclaimed "white witch," who informed Steve she utilized witchcraft only for good. He then reflected back to the Old Testament, where it speaks of the sin of witchcraft:

There shall not be found among you anyone who ... practices witchcraft, or a soothsayer, or one who interprets omens, or a sorcerer, or one who conjures spells, or a medium, or a spiritist, or one who calls up the dead." "For all who do these things are an abomination to the Lord. (Deut. 18:10–12)

Also he caused his sons to pass through the fire in the Valley of the Son of Hinnom; He practiced soothsaying, used witchcraft and sorcery, and consulted mediums and spiritists. He did much evil in the sight of the Lord, to provoke Him to anger. (2 Chron. 33:6)

> For rebellion is as the sin of witchcraft, and stubbornness is as iniquity and idolotry. (1 Sam. 15:23)

Steve paused for a moment. One of the verses began to sear his conscience: "For rebellion is as the sin of witchcraft." *God considers rebellion equally wicked and sinful as witchcraft,* he mused. Dr. Talbott proceeded to grab a standard dictionary from one of the bookshelves. He wanted to look up the definition of "rebellion." The definitions included, "Resistance against or defiance of any authority or control. Act of rebelling." Also listed were synonyms: "Insurrection, mutiny, sedition, revolution, insubordination, disobedience." The last synonym seemed to leap off the page at Steve: "disobedience." *Lord, do You really consider a person's disobedience as sinful and wicked as witchcraft?"* he asked silently. Dr. Talbott reflected on how many times he knowingly and willfully disobeyed God because obedience at the time would have been inconvenient. Though a professed Christian, Steve Talbott often lived his life as if he recited the Lord's Prayer in the following fashion:

> Lord, this time, it's not *Thy* will but *my* will that must be done. I realize what I desire and what I plan to do is against Your Word. Nevertheless, I know You are a God who forgives and understands how much I want to do this. So, Lord, thank you in advance for forgiving me of this trespass. Amen.

God considers willful disobedience wicked and in the same category with witchcraft, he wondered. As Steve considered this passage, he looked up for a brief moment and observed the clock on the library wall. *Good grief, I can't believe it's almost midnight,* he thought. Steve picked up the phone and called Lisa in ICU. "Lisa, how are Allison and Courtney doing?" he asked.

"Not so good" she sadly replied. "None of the treatments thus far are working. Neither Courtney nor Allison have improved. Courtney's spinal fluid results came back negative. She does not have meningitis." Lisa continued, "I just got off the phone with Dr. Andrew's nurse. He's the chairman for the Department of Infectious Disease at University Hospital. I've requested a consultation with him regarding our current treatment plan for Allison and Courtney. I've also placed a call into the Centers for Disease Control requesting their assistance. And Steve, just to let you know, Dr. Martin will be taking over for me for a couple of hours. I'm exhausted. I want to go home and get some shut-eye."

"I think I'll do the same," Steve said in agreement. "By the way Lisa, I'm planning to attend church in the morning. I'll return to the hospital immediately after the service. Will you come to church with me?"

"No, I can't go" she answered emphatically.

"Well then, I'll see you after church. Try and get some sleep," Steve said to her gently. Both doctors left Clarion General Hospital and headed to their respective homes. Steve's body clamored for rest as he slowly crawled into bed. Closing his eyes, his mind began to replay events of the day: *Allison so dehydrated her kidneys have begun to fail. Courtney with a dangerously elevated body temperature. So many sick people from Safe Harbor pouring into the ER. Lab tests all coming back normal. Standard medical treatments are failing. Is it possible witchcraft could be involved in this outbreak?* "*For rebellion is as the sin of witchcraft.*" *God considers a person's disobedience as the sin of witchcraft? In God's eyes, a person's willful disobedience to His Word is as sinful as witchcraft?* Steve Talbott slowly drifted off to sleep.

CHAPTER FIVE

It was now eight o'clock on Sunday morning. Brilliant beams of sunlight traversed a cloudless, azure summer sky, piercing the Victorian stained-glass windows of Clarion Evangelical Church. Inside the hundred-year-old stone edifice, Steve Talbott and the other members of the congregation lifted holy hands as they sang praises to God Almighty and Jesus His Son. The worshippers quieted as Pastor Markham walked to the podium and took his place behind the lectern. "Good morning, fellow believers!" he bellowed. "This is the day that the Lord hath made. Let us rejoice and be glad in it!" More shouts of praise to God echoed throughout the sanctuary. The room again fell silent as Pastor Markham, looking across the crowded room, began to address the people God placed in his charge:

"I know we are all aware and closely following the situation unfolding at Safe Harbor Bible Camp. For the past two days, our community's talented health-care professionals, along with Clarion Health Department officials, have worked tirelessly to find a cure for this dreadful illness. I am told Clarion's medical professionals are indeed challenged by this elusive disease. But, as Christians, we are confident God is neither confused nor perplexed by what is occurring at Safe Harbor Bible Camp. As children of God, we are confident our Heavenly Father remains in perfect control of this situation. I am fully persuaded God will be faithful to reveal the cause of this sickness in His perfect timing.

Yesterday afternoon, my wife, Shelley, and I spent time together, discussing what is happening at Safe Harbor and what investigative efforts have thus far revealed. I listened intently to what Shelley had to say and devoted several hours in prayer, requesting God's help with this challenge to our community. Afterward, I felt led by the Spirit to replace the sermon I intended to deliver this morning with a series of sermons. I believe the topic for this series is far more relevant to what we are witnessing at Safe Harbor and, indeed, even in the world today. I have named the series 'Spiritual Diseases of the Heart.' This morning, I will begin with a very contagious spiritual illness that infects so many believers. It is the disease known as 'Disobedience.' But first, I must challenge each of you with three seemingly irrelevant questions. First, what does the Word of God tell us about the reality of curses? Second, are curses truly able to cause bad things to happen to people? And third, what allows a person to be negatively impacted by a curse? To answer these questions, let us look to what is written in the Holy Bible. I perceive some of you may be thinking, *Come now, Pastor. We live in the twenty-first century. Do you expect me to believe curses are real?*

To answer the first question, I ask that you turn with me to the Old Testament book of Deuteronomy, chapter 10, verses 12 and 13. In this book, through Moses, God makes His expectations abundantly clear to the people of Israel, whom He just delivered out of Egypt to serve Him:

"And now, Israel, what does the Lord your God require of you, but to fear the Lord your God, to walk in all His ways and to love Him, to serve the Lord your God with all your heart and with all your soul, and to keep the commandments of the Lord and His statutes which I command you today for your good?"

"And chapter 11, verse 1: '"Therefore you shall love the Lord your God, and keep His charge, His statutes, His judgments, and His commandments always.'"

"Chapter 12, verse 28 reads: '"Observe and obey all these words which I command you, that it may go well with you and your children after you forever, when you do what is good and right in the sight of the Lord your God."

"In chapter 13, verse 4, one reads, '"You shall walk after the Lord your God and fear Him, and keep His commandments and obey His voice; you shall serve Him and hold fast to Him.'" And in chapter 13, verse 18, '"... to do what is right in the eyes of the Lord your God."'"

"From these few passages alone, there can be no doubt God expects and even demands His people remain faithful to Him and obedient to His commandments. God promises to bless those who keep His commandments but reprimand those who are disobedient through curses. In Deuteronomy 11:26–28 we read:

"Behold, I set before you today a blessing and a curse: the blessing, if you obey the commandments of the Lord your God... and the curse, if you do not obey the commandments of the Lord your God, but turn aside from the way which I command you today.

"God makes it abundantly clear through His servant Moses that He would bless the people who remained obedient His commandments, but allow curses to befall those who were disobedient. How serious was God about allowing curses to afflict those who chose disobedience? Serious enough to enumerate them in Deuteronomy chapters 27 and 28. I shall now read a list of curses to you as written in Scripture:

> Deuteronomy 27:16: "Cursed is the one who treats his father or his mother with contempt."
>
> Deuteronomy 27:19: "Cursed is the one who perverts justice due the stranger, the fatherless, and widow."
>
> Deuteronomy 27:20: "Cursed is the one who lies with his father's wife (incest)."
>
> Deuteronomy27:21: "Cursed is the one who lies with any kind of animal "
>
> Deuteronomy 27:22: "Cursed is the one who lies with his sister, the daughter of his father or the daughter of his mother (incest)."
>
> Deuteronomy 27:24: "Cursed is the one who attacks his neighbor secretly."
>
> Deuteronomy 27:25: :Cursed is the one who takes a bribe to slay an innocent person."

"And in the twenty-eighth chapter of the book of Deuteronomy, we read:

Verse 15: "But it shall come to pass, if you do not obey the voice of the Lord your God, to observe carefully all His commandments and His statutes which I command you today, that all these curses will come upon you and overtake you."

Verse 16: "Cursed shall you be in the city, and cursed shall you be in the country."

Verse 20: "The Lord will send on you cursing, confusion, and rebuke in all that you set your hand to do, until you are destroyed and until you perish quickly, because of the wickedness of your doings in which you have forsaken Me."

Verse 21: "The Lord will make the plague (illness) cling to you until He has consumed you."

Verse 22: "The Lord will strike you with consumption (tuberculosis?), with fever, with inflammation (arthritis?), with severe burning fever, with the sword (war), with scorching, and with mildew; they (the curses) shall pursue you until you perish."

Verse 25: "The Lord will cause you to be defeated before your enemies;... you shall become troublesome to all the kingdoms of the earth. "

Verse 27: "The Lord will strike you with the boils of Egypt, with tumors, with the scab, and with the itch, from which you cannot be healed."

Verse 28: "The Lord will strike you with madness (mental illness) and blindness and confusion of heart."

Verse 30: "You shall betroth a wife, but another man shall lie with her; you shall build a house, but you shall not dwell in it; you shall plant a vineyard, but shall not gather its grapes."

Verse 35: "The Lord will strike you in the knees and on the legs with severe boils which cannot be healed, and from the sole of your foot to the top of your head."

Verse 59: "If you do not carefully observe all the words of this law that are written in this book, that you may fear this glorious and awesome name, THE LORD YOUR GOD, then the Lord will bring upon you and your descendants extraordinary plagues (genetically inherited illnesses?)—great and prolonged plagues—and serious and prolonged sicknesses (cancer? heart disease? diabetes?)."

Verse 60: Moreover, He will bring back on you all the diseases of Egypt, of which you were afraid, and they shall cling to you."

Verse 61: "Also every sickness and every plague, which is not written in this Book of the Law, will the Lord bring upon you until you are destroyed."

Verse 65: " ... the Lord will give you a trembling heart, failing eyes, and anguish of soul (extreme fearfulness? tremendous anxiety?)."

Verse 66: "Your life shall hang in doubt before you; you shall fear day and night, and have no assurance of life."Verse 67: "In the morning you shall say, 'Oh, that it were evening!' And at evening you shall say, 'Oh, that it were morning!' because of the fear which terrifies your heart, and because of the sight which your eyes see."

And in verse 45, "Moreover, all these curses shall come upon you and pursue and overtake you, until you are destroyed, because you did not obey the voice of the

Lord your God, to keep His commandments and His statutes which He commanded you."

"Many more examples of curses can be found in the Bible. In fact, the word 'curse' is mentioned in the Old and New Testaments 194 times. I cannot believe curses are mere figments of the human imagination if cited 194 times in the Bible and if two entire chapters in the book of Deuteronomy are dedicated to enumerating them. Why would God have assigned so many pages of Scripture to describe curses if they were not real or did not exist? Further, we read in Proverbs 26:2, 'Like a flitting sparrow, like a flying swallow, so a curse without cause shall not alight.'

"Would this passage not then imply a curse *with* cause *shall* alight? If we are truly honest with ourselves, it becomes all too clear curses are quite real.

"Next, to answer the second and third questions: Can a curse actually cause bad things to happen? and 'What allows a person to be negatively impacted by a curse?' let us look to the life of David as one example. The Bible tells us although David was a man after God's own heart, God still punished David because of his disobedience. With Bathsheba, David knowingly and deliberately disobeyed the following commandments of God: 'You shall not commit adultery'; 'You shall not covet your neighbor's wife ... nor anything that is your neighbor's'; 'You shall not murder.'

"Why is it that David, so richly blessed and beloved by God, a man who sang psalms of love and praise to his Creator, chose to commit both adultery and murder? Is it not because David placed his will before God's? Did David not choose 'Lord, not thy will but My will be done?' The Bible tells us David secretly arranged for Uriah, Bathsheba's husband and one of David's devoted soldiers, to die in battle. On Uriah's death, David would then take Bathsheba as his wife. In the eleventh chapter of 2 Samuel, verses 14–15, we read:

In the morning it happened that David wrote a letter to Joab and sent it by the hand of Uriah. And he wrote in the letter, saying, "Set Uriah in the forefront of the hottest battle, and retreat from him, that he may be struck down and die."

"And verse 28,

When the wife of Uriah heard that her husband was dead, she mourned for her husband. And when her mourning was over, David sent and brought her to his house, and she became his wife and bore him a son. But the thing that David had done displeased the Lord.

"Then, in 2 Samuel chapter 12, verses 1–12, we read of the serious consequences incurred by David due to his willful disobedience to God:

Then the Lord sent Nathan to David. Then Nathan said to David, "Thus says the Lord God of Israel: 'I anointed you king over Israel, and I delivered you from the hand of Saul. I gave you your master's house and your master's wives into your keeping, and gave you the house of Israel and Judah. And if that had been too little, I also would have given you much more!

'Why have you despised the commandment of the Lord, to do evil in His sight? You have killed Uriah the Hittite with the sword; you have taken his wife to be your wife, and have killed him with the sword of the people of Ammon. Now therefore, the sword shall never depart from your house, because you have despised Me, and have taken the wife of Uriah the Hittite to be your wife.'

"Thus says the Lord: 'Behold, I will raise up adversity against you from your own house; and I will take your wives before your eyes and give them to your neighbor, and he shall lie with your wives in the sight of this sun. For you did it secretly, but I will do this thing before all Israel, before the sun.'"

"We know from reading the remainder of the book of 2 Samuel, David sincerely repented of the sins he committed. And although God forgave David and continued to bless him thereafter, God's punishment stood. David's life was, henceforth, chaotic and lacked the true peace and joy he once knew:

"Second Samuel 12:15–19, David and Bathsheba's firstborn died: 'And the Lord struck the child that Uriah's wife bore to David, and it became ill... Then on the seventh day it came to pass that the child died.'

In 2 Samuel 13: 1–14, we find that David's son, Amnon, raped his sister Tamar: 'Then Amnon said to Tamar, "Bring the food into the bedroom, that I may eat from your hand" ... when she had brought them to him to eat, he took hold of her and said to her, "Come lie with me my sister." But she answered him, "No my brother, do not force me, for no such thing should be done in Israel. Do not do this disgraceful thing!" However, he would not heed her voice; and being stronger than she, he forced her and lay with her."

In 2 Samuel 13:28-31, Absalom, Tamar's brother and David's son, arranged to have his stepbrother, Amnon, killed for raping Tamar: 'Now Absalom had commanded his servants, saying, Watch now, when Amnon's heart is merry with wine, and when I say to you, Strike Amnon! then kill him... So the servants of Absalom did to Amnon as Absalom had commanded... And it came to pass... that news came to David... So the king arose and tore his garments and lay on the ground.'

"In 2 Samuel 15:10–14, we learn that Absalom attempted to steal the throne from his father, David: 'Then Absalom sent spies throughout all the tribes of Israel, saying, As soon as you hear the sound of the trumpet, then you shall say, Absalom reigns in Hebron! ... Now a messenger came to David, saying, The hearts of the men of Israel are with Absalom. So David said to all his servants who were with him at Jerusalem, Arise, and let us flee, or we shall not escape from Absalom. Make haste to depart, lest he overtake us suddenly and bring disaster upon us, and strike the city with the edge of the sword.'

"Absalom planned to have David killed, as found in 2 Samuel 16:11: 'And David said to Abishai and all his servants, See how my son who came from my own body seeks my life.'

"And, as we find out in chapter 18, verses 14 and 15, Absalom was eventually killed in battle: 'Then Joab... took three spears in his hand and thrust them through Absalom's heart... And ten young men who bore Joab's armor surrounded Absalom, and struck and killed him.'

"Do we recognize as a portion of David's punishment some of the very curses I just read from the book of Deuteronomy? 'Cursed is the one who attacks his neighbor secretly.' 'The Lord will strike you with... the sword... they shall pursue you until you perish.' 'The Lord will give you a trembling heart, failing eyes, and anguish of soul.' 'Your life shall hang in doubt before you; you shall fear day and night, and have no assurance of life.'

"Can we see these curses at work in David's life after willfully disobeying God? Do we see the utter chaos and calamity befalling David and his family? Do we understand that when David chose to disobey God by doing his will rather that God's, he stepped out from under God's protective wings? Without the Lord's protection from adversity, David unwittingly exposed himself and his family to a host of curses. In Deuteronomy 11:26–28, God cautions that there is a penalty for not living according to his commandments:

> "Behold, I set before you today a blessing and a curse: the blessing, if you obey the commandments of the Lord your God ... and the curse, if you do not obey the commandments of the Lord your God, but turn aside from the way which I command you."

"Can it be any more obvious? Regardless of how God-loving a person such as David might be, if he or she willfully sins through disobedience, though not always immediate, chastening will follow: 'For whom the Lord loves, He chastens,' found in Hebrews 12:6, and, 'As many as I love, I rebuke and chasten. Therefore, be zealous and repent,' which we read in Revelation 3:19.

"Another example of the negative effects of a curse is when God cursed the cities of Sodom and Gomorrah because, 'the men of Sodom were exceedingly wicked and sinful against the Lord,' which is found in Genesis 13:13. And to this day, neither of the two cities have been rebuilt or resettled because of God's curse. Jeremiah 50:40 reads, 'As God overthrew Sodom and Gomorrah and their neighbors, says the Lord, so no one shall reside there, nor son of man dwell in it.'

"Still another example of what a spoken curse can do is in Matthew 21:18, where we read: 'Now in the morning, as He (Jesus) returned to the city, He was hungry. And seeing the fig tree by the road, He came to it and found nothing on it but leaves, and said to it, "Let no fruit grow on you ever again." Immediately the fig tree withered away.'

"Some of you may be thinking, *These verses of Scripture are simply using the words 'curse' and 'cursing' in the same context we talk about 'cursing,' 'swearing,' and 'foul language.'* I ask you to turn with me to the book of Numbers. In chapter 22, verses 3–7, we read of when the children of Israel camped in the plains of Moab across from Jericho:

And Moab was exceedingly afraid of the people because they were many, and Moab was sick with dread because of the children of Israel. So Moab said to the elders of Midian, "Now this company will lick up everything around us, as an ox licks up the grass of the field." And Balak the son of Zippor was king of the Moabites at that time. Then he (Balak) sent messengers to Balaam the son of Beor ... saying: "Look, a people has come from Egypt. See they cover the face of the earth, and are settling next to me! Therefore please come at once, curse this people for me, for they are too mighty for me. Perhaps I shall be able to defeat them and drive them out of the land, for I know that whom you bless is blessed, and whom you curse is cursed." So the elders of Moab and the elders of Midian departed with the diviner's fee in their hand, and they came to Balaam and spoke to him the words of Balak.

"From our reading thus far, it appears Balak truly believed Balaam, a mortal man, was a soothsayer who used divination and the power of witchcraft to bless or curse people. As we continue to read in Numbers chapter 22, verses 9–12, we see what God's response was to Balak's request of Balaam:

Then God came to Balaam and said "Who are these men with you?" So Balaam said to God, "Balak the son of Zippor, king of Moab, has sent to me, saying, Look, a people has come out of Egypt, and they cover the face of the earth. Come now, curse them for me; perhaps I shall be able to overpower them and drive them out." And God said to Balaam, "You shall not go with them; you shall not curse the people, for they are blessed."

"Had God instructed Balaam not to 'curse at' the people or 'swear at' them, or direct foul language toward them? No! Although God's mighty power can defeat any curse produced by witchcraft, through His infinite wisdom, God commanded Balaam not to attempt to place a curse on His people through divination. Why? Because He had already blessed them. There are many more verses of Scripture, both Old and New Testament, that refer to curses. However, we do not have the time this morning to address them all. But, before we continue, I will read five more verses referring to curses:

> Psalm 109:17: "As he loved cursing, so let it come to Him; As he did not delight in blessing, so let it be far from him."
>
> Malachi 3:9: "'You are cursed with a curse, for you have robbed Me.'"
>
> Hebrews 6:7–8: "For the earth which drinks in the rain that often comes upon it, and bears herbs useful for those by whom it is cultivated, receives blessing from God; but if it bears thorns and briers, it is rejected and near to being cursed, whose end is to be burned."
>
> Second Peter 14–15: "... having eyes full of adultery and that cannot cease from sin, enticing unstable souls. They have a heart trained in covetous practices, and are accursed children. They have forsaken the right way and gone astray, following the way of Baalam."

James 3:9–10: "With it (the tongue) we bless our God and Father, and with it we curse men... Out of the same mouth proceed blessing and cursing."

"We have, up to this point, talked about curses, the reality of curses, and the effects of curses on both people and events portrayed in Scripture. But, how does all this pertain to us living in the twenty-first century? How can curses adversely affect us as believers? As followers of Jesus Christ, we are washed white as snow, redeemed by His shed blood. To this I say, 'Yes, Yes, and Amen!' But, does our being saved from hell mean if we deliberately disobey God, no harm or consequences will come to us? 'But Pastor,' you ask, 'what about the promise of Psalm 91, verses 10 and 11, where it says: "Because you have made the Lord... your dwelling place, no evil shall befall you, nor shall any plague come near your dwelling; For He shall give His angels charge over you."'

"To this I answer, have you truly made the Lord your dwelling place? Do you pray daily? Are you obedient to God's Word? Do you love your neighbor as you love yourself? Do you obey the Ten Commandments of God, or do you consider them mere suggestions? Do you truly live your life by what is written in Psalm 91 in order to receive God's promise of protection by calling upon the Lord daily? By setting your love upon Him over self-love and self-desire? Do you have a strong desire to please Him by your actions? Do you ever consider how you may be grieving God's heart by your disobedience? Do you pray and truly mean, 'Lord, Thy will be done rather than my will.' But now you may ask about the book of Galatians, where it tells us in chapter 3, verse 13, we are no longer under the curse of Old Testament law. 'Christ has redeemed us from the curse of the law, having become a curse for us (for it is written, "Cursed is everyone who hangs on a tree")'

"To this, I respond with Galatians 5:13–16: 'For you, brethren, have been called to liberty; only do not use liberty as an opportunity for the flesh... I say then: Walk in the Spirit, and you shall not fulfill the lust of the flesh.'

"Yes, we live in a time of grace through Christ our Lord and Savior's atoning sacrifice for us. But, does His sacrifice allow us the freedom to do whatever we please, because God will surely forgive us? If our desire is contrary to the Word of God and we act on that desire in frank disobedience, will God hold us blameless with no questions asked? What kind of loving parent would allow a child to deliberately break rules that were established for the child's welfare? Do we expect then a Holy God will abstain from chastening us, the children He loves? If God did not correct us, what manner of Heavenly Father would He be? But, many Christians would then argue per Romans 8:1, 'There is therefore now no condemnation to those who are in Christ Jesus.'

"These people seem to forget the second half of this verse, 'who do not walk according to the flesh, but according to the Spirit.'

"How many professed Christians have at times walked according to their own fleshly desires? How many of us have done 'little things' God would consider 'insignificant' and 'ignore,' such as stealing pens and other office supplies from our employers? How many men and women claiming to be followers of Jesus Christ in disobedience to the Lord have cheated on their income tax, thereby robbing Caesar?

Who among us has lusted in his or her heart for another sexually? How many Christians have acted on their fleshly desires either while unmarried, thereby committing fornication, or if married to another participating in the sin of adultery? How many Christians have become addicted to drugs and alcohol, pornography, or gambling? How many believers have become idolaters, lusting after material things the world has to offer rather than desiring the spiritual things God offers us? Many exhortations are found throughout the pages of Scripture that caution us not to engage in activities contrary to God's Will. Brothers and sisters in Christ, grievous to us can be the consequences of willful disobedience!

"I will now read from Scripture some exhortations along with their consequences:

> Romans 13:14: "But put on the Lord Jesus Christ, and make no provision for the flesh, to fulfill its lusts."
>
> Hebrews 13:4: "Marriage is honorable among all, and the (marital) bed undefiled; but fornicators and adulterers God will judge."
>
> Colossians 3:5–6: "Therefore put to death... fornication, uncleanness, passion, evil desire, and covetousness, which is idolatry. Because of these things the wrath of God is coming upon the sons of disobedience."
>
> Second Peter 2:20–21: "For if, after they have escaped the pollutions of the world through the knowledge of the Lord and Savior Jesus Christ, they are again entangled in them and overcome (with sin), the latter end is worse for them than the beginning. For it would

have been better for them not to have known the way of righteousness, than having known it, to turn from the holy commandment delivered to them."

Luke 12:40–47: "Therefore you also be ready for the Son of Man is coming at an hour you do not expect... But if that servant says in his heart, 'My master is delaying his coming,' and begins to beat the male and female servants, and to eat and drink and be drunk, the master of that servant will come on a day when he is not looking for him, and at an hour when he is not aware, and will cut him in two and appoint his portion with the unbelievers. And that servant who knew his master's will, and did not prepare himself or do according to his will, shall be beaten with many stripes."

John 14–15: "'If you love Me, keep My commandments.'"

Colossians 3:25: "But he who does wrong will be repaid for what he has done, and there is no partiality."

Revelation 21:8: "'He who overcomes shall inherit all things, and I will be his God and he shall be My son. But the cowardly, unbelieving, abominable, murderers, sexually immoral, sorcerers, idolaters, and all liars shall have their part in the lake which burns with fire and brimstone.'"

Revelation 22:14–15: "Blessed are those who do His commandments, that they may have the right to the tree of life, and may enter through the gates into the city. But outside are dogs and sorcerers and sexually immoral and murderers and idolaters, and whoever loves and practices a lie."

1 John 3:6–8: "Whoever abides in Him does not sin. Whoever sins has neither seen Him nor known Him... He who sins is of the devil."

"It is a fearful thing to fall into the hands of the living God." Hebrews 10:26–31

"Many in the pulpit today eagerly preach of God's abundant goodness, and rightly so! But sadly, few have the courage to speak of the severity of God. In Romans 11:22, we find, 'Therefore consider the goodness and severity of God: on those who fell, severity; but toward you, goodness, if you continue in His goodness. Otherwise, you also will be cut off.' In Isaiah 9:16, it is written, 'For the leaders of this people (some members of today's clergy?) cause them to err, and those who are led by them are destroyed.' And in Hosea 4:6, 'My people are destroyed for lack of knowledge.'

"Yes, many of God's people are destroyed for lacking the knowledge of what God expects of His children. Why? Perhaps because they spend so little time in prayer and reading His Word. Or, perhaps because so many of our religious leaders today spend more time preaching the 'gospel of prosperity' rather than reminding us how important it is to remain obedient to God's Word and live a holy life! Remember what Jesus teaches us in Matthew 6:33, 'But seek first the kingdom of God and His righteousness, and all these things shall be added to you.'

"Brothers and sisters, this morning's sermon has been about the spiritual disease known as disobedience and its spiritual cure— obedience. We must remain obedient to God's every Word or suffer the consequences. Whereas obedience brings the blessings of God into a person's life, disobedience eventually meets with disaster, as witnessed by what happened to David. Willful disobedience to God opens doors for Satan and his demon horde to attack by way of disease, depression, financial disaster, marital or family discord, and yes, even through witchcraft and curses. Your eternal destiny may well depend on being obedient to God. Where in the pages of Scripture does it say, 'All you have to do is recite the prayer of faith, and you'll go straight to Heaven'? Or, 'Don't worry about daily Bible reading, or prayer, or obedience to God's Word. Just say the sinner's prayer, and brother, you're going to Heaven when you die.' No! No! For Heaven's sake, no! The Bible makes it abundantly clear in 1 John 2:4: 'He who says, "I know Him," and does not keep His commandments, is a liar, and the truth is not in him.'

"Revelation 21:8 also emphasizes no liar will enter the kingdom of Heaven:

> "He who overcomes shall inherit all things, and I will be his God and he shall be My son. But the cowardly, unbelieving, abominable, murderers, sexually immoral, sorcerers, idolaters, and all liars shall have their part in the lake which burns with fire and brimstone."

"More frightening, the Bible teaches in Matthew 7:21–23, not all those who claim to be Christians will gain entrance into Heaven:

> "Many will say to Me in that day, 'Lord, Lord, have we not prophesied in Your name, cast out demons in Your name, and done many wonders in Your name?' And then

I will declare to them, 'I never knew you; depart from Me, you who practice lawlessness!'"

"Who is Jesus speaking to in this passage? Is He speaking to unbelievers who could care less about prophesying, or casting out demons, or doing wonders in His glorious name? No! The Lord is speaking to believers! Fellow Christians, do not allow yourselves to be destroyed for lacking knowledge of what is written in the Word of God! Do not allow yourselves to miss out on Heaven because of willful disobedience to God's Word and to His commandments! Do not give heed to fables and false teachers! Do not believe false doctrine like the 'prosperity gospel,' preached ad nauseum and promulgated by so many in the pulpit today! Rather, focus on how to live a holy life in obedience to a loving and Holy God.

"Dear brothers and sisters, when the time comes to stand before the Lord, I pray none of us here this morning will have to confess these words of Jeremiah 18:12 to Him: 'So we will walk (walked) according to our own plans, and we will every one obey (obeyed) the dictates of his evil heart.' Or from Judges 17:6, 'Everyone did what was right in his own eyes.' Or Proverb 14:12, 'There is a way which seems (seemed) right to a man, but its end is the way of death.'

"It is my fervent hope and heartfelt desire our Lord Jesus will say something like this to each and every believer on that day:

My child, I have loved you with an everlasting love and have been with you in all your times of trial and suffering. You have been faithful to persevere. You have loved Me with all your heart and remained obedient to God's Word until the very end. You have completed your race and have kept the faith. And now I say to you, My precious child, well done good and faithful servant. Come enter into My Heavenly rest."

Having concluded his sermon, Pastor Markham raised his arms skyward. With a loud voice and angelic smile, he said to his congregation, "Now go with God this Lord's day, dear people of God, and be blessed!" Worshippers of Clarion Evangelical Church quietly and reverently exited the sanctuary. As he watched his flock leave the church, the pastor could not help wonder how many would heed his message? How many would turn from "self-desire" to obeying "His desire"? How many hearts would catch fire with a renewed commitment to live their lives in obedience, well-pleasing to God?

CHAPTER SIX

Dr. Talbott sprinted down the worn, cobblestone steps of the church. As he descended, Steve turned and waved good-bye to Pastor Markham. Jeremy was now outside the church, standing at the top of the steps and talking with members of his congregation. Anxious to get back to the hospital, Dr. Talbott hurried into his car, parked in the lot behind the church. As he drove toward Clarion General, Steve could not help but meditate on all that Pastor Markham preached during his sermon. The thought that witchcraft and curses could be the cause of the outbreak at Safe Harbor haunted him. *Could curses be playing a role at Safe Harbor? Are these people becoming ill through disobedience to God as Pastor Jeremy suggested? Why, then, are only some getting sick? If we are all sinners, falling short of the glory of God, if we all disobey at times, why haven't all at the camp gotten sick?*

In fifteen minutes, Dr. Talbott pulled his car into the hospital parking lot near the main entrance. He rode the elevator to the third floor, where the ICU was located. Steve spotted Lisa seated behind the cardiac monitor console. She appeared fatigued, and her face wore a look of concern. Sitting down beside her, Steve inquired as to the status of Allison and Courtney. Pointing to the monitor, Lisa informed him Allison had continued to deteriorate throughout the night. Now, with her kidneys failing, she was deemed critically ill and would require dialysis if she did not quickly improve. Dr.

Sommers expressed concern Allison might not survive another forty-eight hours. Courtney, on the other hand, had begun to stabilize. Her fever now ranged between 101 degrees and 102 degrees, down from the 105 degrees previously registered on the thermometer. Additionally, Lisa informed Steve that Dr. Andrew from University Hospital contacted her earlier that morning. Dr. Andrew felt the treatment being provided to Allison and Courtney was appropriate and consistent with the standards of care. Unfortunately, he did not have any further suggestions regarding their treatment. The CDC personnel had not yet gotten back to Lisa.

Shaking his head in dismay, Steve got up from his chair to look in on the two women. Glancing into Allison's room through the sliding glass door, Steve observed a man standing at her bedside with his back to the door. "Lisa, who is Allison's visitor?" Steve queried.

"I didn't notice anyone go in to see her," Lisa replied. As he stood in the doorway, Steve saw the man's left hand was positioned over the sleeping Allison's forehead, while his right hand was directly on top of her abdomen. He was whispering something in Allison's ear. As Dr. Talbott opened the glass door, he startled Allison's guest.

"Hello sir. My name is Dr. Talbott. I'm here to see how Allison is doing."

"Oh, uh, good morning. Sorry, Dr. Talbott. You startled me. I'm Allison's fiancé, James Clayw—uh, Jim Worth."

"Oh, Mr. Worth! Allison told me all about you the other night, while she was being treated in the ER. She spoke of how the two of you met last summer at Safe Harbor and are now engaged to be married."

"That's correct," Jim answered, his face void of emotion.

"Well, I'd like to congratulate you."

"Thanks," Jim blandly replied.

Steve continued, "Allison asked if you and I were acquainted. She told me you're a native of Clarion but recently moved to Iowa."

"Uh yeah, that's right. I moved from Clarion a few years ago to participate in something I couldn't pass up."

"What line of work are you in?" Steve asked.

"I really don't want to discuss that now," Jim replied.

"I apologize, Mr. Worth. I didn't mean to pry. I'm terribly sorry to inform you Allison is not doing very well," Dr. Talbott reported. "Dr. Lisa Sommers, from our hospital's Infectious Disease Department, has been taking care of her. At this time, we are still unable to determine the reason Allison is so critically ill. The medications Dr. Sommers prescribed to help control Allison's vomiting and diarrhea have not proven effective. Now, Allison's kidneys have begun to shut down, and she may soon require dialysis. Dr. Sommers consulted with Dr. Andrew, a specialist at University Hospital, regarding Allison's condition. Unfortunately, he has no additional suggestions to help us treat her. I wish there were better news, but I must be candid when reporting Allison's condition to you. Mr. Worth, are there any questions I can answer for you at this time?" Steve asked with concern.

"No, I don't have any questions right now. Just do what you can for her," Jim replied. "Oh, I do have one question," he said in a humdrum voice. "Is the hospital cafeteria open yet? I'm hungry, and I want to get some food."

"Yes, it's open," Steve replied, gazing at Worth with disdain. "The cafeteria is located on the main floor of the hospital, across from the elevators. Mr. Worth, I can have a tray brought to you if you would like to remain here with Allison."

"No thanks. I'd rather go down to the cafeteria." Jim then nonchalantly left Allison's bedside and headed toward the elevator.

Steve went out to the cardiac monitor console and sat beside Lisa. "He's a strange man," Steve muttered. "Do you know him, Lisa? His name is Jim Worth. He's from Clarion."

"Nope. I've never met the guy," Lisa responded as she continued to study Allison's heartbeat on the monitor.

Just then, a nurse from pediatrics entered the ICU, holding a little girl's hand. The girl was dressed in a light blue patient gown and clung to her teddy bear. Dr. Talbott immediately rose from his chair and walked to the little girl, giving her a big hug. "Lizzie! How are you feeling?" he asked with a wide grin.

"I'm all better!" Lizzie replied. "Can I see my mommy now? Is Mommy all better, too? I prayed for her to get better," she declared.

"Yes, Lizzie." "Your mommy is doing much better," Steve responded. Taking Lizzie's little hand, he said, "Why don't we both go in to see her?"

"Okay," she giggled, smiling. As the two entered Courtney's room, Steve noticed that although she appeared quite pale, Courtney was propped up in bed, and slowly sipping hot tea. "Mommy!" Lizzie shouted, grasping one of Courtney's hands.

"Hi sweetie," Courtney replied weakly, smiling at her beloved daughter.

"I missed you, Mommy, and I prayed that God would make you feel better!"

"Oh, thanks, honey," Courtney said, gently squeezing Lizzie's hand.

"Mommy, can we go home now?" the little girl asked expectantly.

"No, not yet, sweetie," Steve answered, "but soon. Mommy still has to get a little bit better," he explained.

"Okay, Doctor," Lizzie replied disappointedly.

"But Lizzie, you can come here to see your mommy anytime you want," Steve said, smiling. "Courtney, I'm glad to see you're improving. You had us a little worried."

"Thanks, Dr. Talbott. I do feel better, especially now that my sweet Lizzie came to visit me."

"Mommy, I want to pray for you before I go back to my room." Without waiting for Courtney's response, Lizzie got down onto her knees beside her mommy's bed and prayed, "Dear God, thank you for making my mommy better. And thank you for making me all better, too. Please make her all better now so we can go home from the hospital. Thank you, God. Love, Lizzie."

"Oh, to possess Lizzie's childlike faith," Steve mused, smiling. He took Lizzie's hand and guided her to the pediatric nurse waiting by the ICU entrance. The nurse escorted Lizzie back to her room.

Steve walked to where Lisa was seated. He asked if she obtained Allison's final stool culture results. Lisa informed Steve the final culture proved negative for all infectious etiologies. "Well, now we know Allison's illness is not microbial in nature," he whispered. At the same time, one of the ICU nurses approached Dr. Talbott. "Doctor, Joe Jenkins from hospital security is on the phone for you, line one."

"Hospital security? Why does he want to talk to me?" Steve picked up the phone. "This is Dr. Talbott."

"Hello, Dr. Talbott. This is Joe... Joe Jenkins from hospital security. Sorry to bother you, but I have to ask you a question. As I was doing my morning security check a few minutes ago, I found a man wandering around down in the basement. He didn't see me, but I watched him snoop around for a few minutes to see what he had in mind. I eventually ordered him out of an empty storage room. He says his name is Jim Worth. When I asked him what he was doing down there, he said he was looking for the cafeteria. He said you told him it was in the basement. The guy mentioned he was here visiting his fiancée in intensive care. Just wanted to call you to confirm his story."

After taking a few seconds to gather his thoughts, Steve replied, "Mr. Jenkins, thanks for inquiring. Yes, Jim's fiancée is a patient in ICU. He was up here visiting with Allison a few minutes ago. But, I specifically informed him the cafeteria was on the main floor of the hospital. I never directed Mr. Worth to the basement."

"Thanks, Doctor. I'll take care of the rest." After replacing the receiver, Jenkins looked Jim Worth squarely in the eyes and said, "Dr. Talbott confirmed your fiancée, Allison, is a patient up in the ICU. But, Doc never told you the cafeteria was down here in the basement."

"I'm sorry, Mr. Jenkins. I misunderstood the doctor. Please point me in the right direction."

Jenkins then said in a serious voice, "The cafeteria is on the main floor of the hospital, opposite those elevators." Pointing to the bank of elevators a few feet away, Joe added, "Just take one of those up a floor, and you'll find the cafeteria. And Mr. Worth, for future reference, no patients or visitors are allowed in this basement."

"Thank you, Mr. Jenkins. I'll make a mental note of it so there won't be a next time." Jenkins waited for Worth to enter the elevator before continuing with his security rounds.

Steve told Lisa of his telephone conversation with Jenkins. "Very bizarre," he said. "Jim Worth told Joe Jenkins I directed him to the basement to find the hospital cafeteria."

"Steve, this guy Worth is a strange bird."

"Well, I guess it takes all kinds," he responded with a smirk. "Lisa, not to change the subject, but I'd like to discuss with you what Pastor Markham preached in his sermon this morning."

"Steve, I told you I don't believe in that Higher Power stuff. How can there be a Higher Authority in charge when there is so much chaos on earth? Murders, rapes, impending financial collapse, terrorism, threats of nuclear annihilation, good people dying tragically. Shall I go on?"

"Lisa, no one can deny what is happening in the world today. But, I believe it's all part of God's Higher Plan." She shrugged her shoulders and gave Steve the "I totally disagree" look. "But," he said, "let's save that talk for another time." Steve continued, "I'd like to talk to you about the supernatural. Specifically, witchcraft and curses."

"Friend, now I *know* you've gone off your rocker. Steve, you've finally lost it," she said, smiling but with a look of curiosity.

"Lisa, I know as physicians we're trained to act on the basis of scientific evidence and fact. But, we were also encouraged by mentors to keep an open mind about things we may not initially be able to explain based purely on science." Eyes rolling back, Lisa nodded in agreement, while instructing Steve to "proceed."

Steve began to summarize all that Pastor Jeremy articulated in his sermon: obedience to God, consequences of disobedience by stepping out from under God's protective wings, God's blessings and curses as written in Deuteronomy, David's life having become cursed through disobedience to God, and the reality of witchcraft as mentioned in Scripture. Lisa listened intently as Steve described to her portions of the sermon. *Thank God, I think she may actually be taking an interest,* he thought. Lisa sat up in her chair when Steve brought up the topic of curses and witchcraft. "Lisa, is it possible these people at Safe Harbor are being cursed by someone or by some group that despises Christians? We've all read and heard stories about the effects of voodoo curses and hexes placed on individuals in the third world? Even the Bible refers to the reality of witchcraft and curses. Why couldn't it happen to people here who have walked away from God's protection through disobedience?"

"Steve, I'm overwhelmed! You have given me quite a bit to think about and sort out, even in my own life. Yes, I would like to meet your friend Pastor Markham."

"Lisa, I'd be happy to arrange a meeting between the two of you. I'd be *very* happy to arrange it!"

Just then, an announcement came over the hospital's public address system: "There is a black pickup, license plate JIM 666, illegally parked in front of the hospital loading dock. Will the owner of the vehicle please move it from the area immediately, or it will be towed."

Shortly after the announcement, a woman approached the vehicle. She was greeted by security officer Joe Jenkins. "Is this your truck, ma'am?"

"Yes, I'm here to move it."

Jenkins studied the woman's face and said, "Don't you work here in the hospital?"

"Yes, I'm one of the ER nurses. My name is Marisa."

"Is this your pickup, Marisa?" Jenkins inquired.

"Yes, sir," she again replied.

"May I ask why you parked your vehicle in front of the loading area?"

"Oh, my husband probably parked it here temporarily. He went to see his sick cousin up in the ICU. Allison is very ill."

"Visiting his *cousin*, you say?" Joe queried.

"Yes, sir," Marisa replied.

"Is your husband's name Jim Worth?" Joe asked.

"Yes sir, it is."

Pointing to the bed of the truck, Jenkins asked, "What are you hauling under that tarp?"

"Oh," Marisa replied, "my husband does woodworking as a hobby. He's probably just delivering a piece he sold to a customer here in town."

"Please move the vehicle and inform your husband not to park in this area again, not for any reason."

"I'll tell him," Marisa answered, smiling.

"The security department is very busy today," Steve mentioned to Lisa, waiting to hear if there would be any more announcements. "Getting back to our conversation, Lisa, my question to you is this. Since all patient testing is coming back normal—X-rays, scans, labs, cultures—all normal, and since standard treatment has proved ineffective, could curses be impacting these people at Safe Harbor? And if so, would it be worth trying alternative remedies from the Bible?"

"Now you're talking about Bible cures? Okay, Steve, it's time for me to go." With that, Lisa got up from her chair and left the ICU. She wanted to take a short break and get a cup of coffee. But what Lisa truly desired was some time alone to reflect on all that she and Steve had discussed.

After Lisa stepped out, Steve immediately picked up the phone to call Pastor Markham. *Perhaps*, he thought, *Jeremy might have some insight or knowledge as to alternative Bible cures as intimated in Scripture. What a perfect opportunity for Lisa and Pastor Markham to meet*, Steve thought as he proceeded to call Jeremy. "Hello, Markham residence" the pastor answered.

"Hi, Jeremy. This is Steve Talbott."

"Hello, Steve. Did you enjoy this morning's sermon?" Pastor Markham inquired.

"Yes, I found it absolutely intriguing. It was also timely and quite pertinent. In fact, Jeremy, that's why I'm calling you. One of my colleagues and I are eager to meet with you regarding the Safe Harbor outbreak. Lisa and I were discussing whether illnesses caused by curses could potentially be treated with cures mentioned in the Bible?"

"A very interesting concept," Pastor Jeremy replied. "I recall reading Ezekiel 47:12, a verse that speaks to us about healing waters flowing from the Temple:

> Along the bank of the river, on this side and that, will grow all kinds of trees used for food; their leaves will not wither, and their fruit will not fail. They will bear fruit every month, because their water flows from the sanctuary. Their fruit will be for food, and their leaves for medicine.

"But Steve," Pastor Markham cautioned, "it is vital that spiritual healing first precede physical healing. A person must first make himself right with God. He must ask God for forgiveness of his sins and then truly repent. He must obey God and submit to His every Word. A repentant person's prayer can no longer be 'My will be done.' It must now be 'Thy will be done.' Remember, the root word in selfish is 'self.' And yes, I will gladly meet with you and Lisa tonight at my home for further discussion."

"Thanks, Jeremy. Lisa and I will be over later this afternoon. Good-bye.

When Lisa returned to the ICU, she sat down next to Steve. He was on the computer, searching for information related to "Bible cures for various illnesses." Steve paid close attention to remedies relating to Allison's vomiting and diarrhea, Courtney's extreme headaches and dizziness, and treatments for asthma-related symptoms Lizzie had experienced. Intrigued after reading the list of some Bible cures Steve jotted down, Lisa asked, "Are these treatments actually written in the Bible?"

"According to the information I perused and from books I read years ago regarding the topic, they are indeed. And I believe they deserve our consideration," he added.

"But," Lisa remarked, "as physicians, we cannot recommend these treatments to our patients, even though they seem interesting."

"That's true," Steve replied.

Steve told Lisa he spoke with Jeremy Markham after she stepped out of the ICU. "I asked Jeremy if he had time to meet with us this evening, and he agreed. Are you interested?"

"Yes, I'm actually very eager to meet him," Lisa replied.

"Well, we have a few hours before we go over there," Steve said. "Let's go down to the cafeteria to discuss the treatment plan for our patients. Oh, and Lisa, I'll even buy you something to eat!"

"Steve, you never cease to amaze me. What a big spender you are," she said, giggling. Grabbing Steve's arm, the two made their way down to the main floor of the hospital.

Entering the cafeteria, Steve and Lisa saw Devin Matsen seated at a table, eating a sandwich. At an adjacent table, Jim Worth was sipping coffee and conversing with Devin. The two walked over to greet Devin and Jim. "Well, what is a Clarion public health official doing in the hospital cafeteria on Sunday?" Steve asked, chuckling. He added, "Do public officials actually work on weekends?"

"Absolutely not," Devin chimed in with a friendly grin. "I was just in the neighborhood and thought I'd stop here for something to eat," he jested.

"I didn't realize you gentlemen knew each other," Lisa asked.

"We don't," Jim glibly responded. "We just met. Just some small talk."

Lisa then asked, "Would you two care to join us?

"No thanks," Worth replied as he picked up his newspaper. "I want to finish reading this before I get back to Allison." Lisa glanced angrily at Steve as if to ask, "Does this guy care about Allison at all?"

"Devin, would you like to join us?" Lisa asked.

"No thanks, Dr. Sommers. I can't today. I really do have to get to the office. I'm working on a project this weekend. But, I'd like a rain check." Finished with his sandwich, Devin got up from the table. "I will catch you two another time. Oh, and Dr. Talbott," Devin added, "please be careful not to trip over anymore piles of leaves. They can be hazardous!" Smiling, Devin said good-bye to Steve and Lisa and walked out of the cafeteria. Jim quickly grabbed his newspaper and followed Devin.

"What is with this guy Worth?" Lisa questioned. "Does Allison truly intend to marry him?"

"Lisa, we're taught not to judge others, but if I were Allison, I would reconsider," Steve responded.

"I'm curious as to why Devin and Jim left so abruptly," Lisa said.

"Well, Dr. Sommers, it's obviously your perfume!"

"Very funny, Talbott, very funny," she retorted, playfully jabbing Steve in his ribs. After their friendly bantering, the two had something to eat. During their meal, Steve and Lisa talked about how to best treat Allison's and Courtney's medical conditions. They considered various options but could not come to consensus. They were still unable to determine the cause of the problem. Steve continued to ponder the possibility a curse could be the etiology.

"Lisa, I'd like to question some of our Safe Harbor patients as to where they are spiritually. If we can ascertain how close they are walking with the Lord, we might be able to gain more of a perspective as to whether curses are at work here."

"Steve, you go right ahead with that witchcraft stuff. I will continue to focus on the medical aspects of this outbreak and possible causes."

"I'm very anxious to hear what Pastor Jeremy has to say about all this from a biblical perspective," Steve remarked.

"Speaking of which," Lisa cautioned while gazing at her watch, "we had better leave now for the Markham residence, or we'll be late for our meeting with Jeremy."

The two got up from the table and headed back to ICU. They wanted to make a final check on Allison and Courtney before leaving the premises. After a brief evaluation, Steve and Lisa rode the elevator back down to the main floor. As the elevator door opened, they noticed a small crowd congregated in the lobby, near the exit. As the two doctors approached the throng, they observed the reason for the commotion. Security officer Joe Jenkins was in the process of subduing querulous Jim Worth, who was now in handcuffs. At that moment, a police vehicle pulled up to the lobby entrance. Steve and Lisa could see Chief Doyle step out of the squad car. As Doyle entered the fray, he informed Jenkins the Clarion Police Department did not have a reason to arrest Worth. "The police dispatcher told me why we were notified to come to the hospital. And Mr. Jenkins, I'm here to inform you there is no legal justification for us to arrest this man."

"But Chief Doyle," Jenkins responded, "this is the second time today I caught this guy snooping around in the basement of the hospital. I gave him a warning earlier today about trespassing. He also illegally parked his pickup in front of the hospital loading dock. His wife moved it for him. Now, just a few minutes ago, I found the truck illegally parked there again."

"I'm sorry, Mr. Jenkins, but there is nothing I can do. This is an internal matter involving Clarion General Hospital, not the police department. Please remove the handcuffs from this man, or I will have to arrest you for assault and battery." Visibly upset, Jenkins reluctantly removed the handcuffs from Jim Worth. After dispersing the crowd, Chief Doyle looked at Worth and with a stern voice ordered him into his squad car for a "little chat." The two men then stepped into the chief's car and drove off. Jenkins angrily slapped the handcuffs back onto his duty belt and then continued with his rounds. Steve and Lisa looked at each other dumbfounded. They hurriedly got into Steve's car and exited the parking lot, now late for their meeting with Pastor Jeremy.

CHAPTER SEVEN

Still stunned by the incident, Steve and Lisa recounted what they had just witnessed the entire ride to the Markham home. After Steve knocked on the door, Pastor Markham welcomed his two guests and invited them into the study for tea and biscuits. Steve apologized to Jeremy for his tardiness and introduced Lisa. They gave Jeremy a narrative of what transpired in the hospital lobby. "Jimmy Clayworth? When did he get back into town?" Pastor Markham asked.

"Don't you mean Jim Worth?" Lisa asked. "You know, Steve chimed, when I first met Jim in the ICU, he introduced himself as Jim Clayw..., then immediately said Jim Worth." "It was as if he caught himself in a lie." "I never really thought about it until now."

"I guess you two don't know," Jeremy replied. "Jim changed his name years ago to try and hide his identity. He said he wanted to get a new start on life." Pastor Markham continued, "Jim Clayworth and I attended Sunday school together as kids. For years, the Clayworth family belonged to Clarion Evangelical Church while my dad was senior pastor. But, throughout Jim's teenage years, he continually got into trouble with the police. Jimmy was arrested several times for shoplifting, burglary, auto theft, and even armed robbery. His family eventually stopped coming to church after Jim was caught by the Rayburns, breaking into their home. Mr. and Mrs. Rayburn were very warm and kind individuals, missionaries supported by our church. I think the embarrassment from that incident was the final straw for the Clayworth family. Jim eventually changed his name and left for Iowa several years ago. The last I heard, he became involved in some sort of cult activity."

Lisa's eyes widened as she thought about what Jeremy just mentioned. "Is it possible Jim Clayworth or Worth may be involved with what is occurring at Safe Harbor?" she asked.

"An interesting observation," Steve and Jeremy stated simultaneously. The three continued in conversation for almost an hour. It was as though they had been acquainted for years and were old friends. Pastor Markham had a gift for making people feel at home with his friendly demeanor and warm smile. "Well, I suppose we should get down to the matter at hand," Jeremy stated in a more serious tone. "How may I be of help?"

Steve began by telling him, "Lisa and I realize you are acquainted with what is happening at Safe Harbor and with some of our patients. Conventional treatments have failed, and many of the patients are growing worse by the day. I listened intently to your sermon this morning and conveyed much of the information to Lisa. I believe these people are somehow experiencing the effects of a curse. I do not understand why some are being affected while others are not. It is also unclear to me why little Lizzie has completely recovered, her mother, Courtney, appears to be improving, but Allison is near death and will succumb without dialysis. I've read about some cures from the Bible and wondered whether they might be of help in this situation. Lisa, on the other hand, continues to express skepticism and intends to pursue standard treatment modalities." Steve continued, "Jeremy, we would like you to share your thoughts as to what may be occurring and how to proceed. Lisa and I recognize we are running out of options and that some patients may die without immediate intervention."

Gathering his thoughts, Pastor Markham leaned forward in his chair. Looking at Lisa, he began to speak. "Earlier today, Steve and I briefly discussed the possibility some of the herbal remedies mentioned in Scripture could provide relief to your patients. I do not doubt these Bible cures might help ameliorate some of their physical symptoms. But, it is important to understand the root cause of the illness afflicting these people at Safe Harbor. There are many causes of disease. As physicians, you are undoubtedly aware diseases can occur from physiological or infectious etiologies. Some are due to endocrine dysfunction, and others may be the result of familial or inherited disorders. But, at times, physical symptoms can actually stem from a spiritual disorder. What is so vital to comprehend is sinful behavior opens doors for all sorts of evil to enter and wreak havoc in a person's life. Whether an attack comes through Satan, witchcraft, demonic activity, or curses is irrelevant. What we must keep in mind is sinful behavior and disobedience to God opens doors for all proverbial hell to break loose, including affliction through disease. The Bible warns us in 1 Peter 5:8, 'Be sober, be vigilant; because your adversary the devil walks about like a roaring lion, seeking whom he may devour.'

"Also important to remember is that physical symptoms of disease from a spiritual cause must be treated with a spiritual cure. Herbs or prescription medication may help alleviate some of the ailments, but, they do not have the ability to treat the reason for the physical symptoms, namely, the spiritual disease itself."

Lisa asked, "Pastor Markham, are you suggesting a spiritual disease may lead to signs and symptoms similar to a naturally contracted disease?"

"That is exactly what I am suggesting," Jeremy replied.

Lisa then queried, "What are some of these spiritual diseases?"

Jeremy commented, "Some common spiritual diseases infecting a majority of people include disobedience, anger, bitterness, lack of forgiveness, resentment, rejection, and indifference toward God."

Lisa further questioned, "What are some of the physical symptoms caused by these spiritual diseases?"

"Over time," Pastor Markham continued, "spiritual diseases such as anger, bitterness, and resentment can sometimes lead to chronic migraines, irritable bowel syndrome, and even arthritis or fibromyalgia. In Proverbs, the following verses link emotion and physical health: Proverbs 17:22: 'A merry heart does good, like medicine, But a broken spirit dries the bones.' (Does this refer to arthritis?); Proverbs 15:30: 'The light of the eyes rejoices the heart, And a good report makes the bones healthy'; and Proverbs 16:24: 'Pleasant words are like a honeycomb, Sweetness to the soul and health to the bones.'"

Jeremy continued. "Another common spiritual disease, lack of forgiveness, can lead to an entire host of problems, including physical illness. In Matthew chapter 18, verses 32–35, Jesus tells a parable of the wicked servant. Though the servant's master forgave him of his debt, the servant refused to forgive others of the debt they owed him. Jesus warned of the consequences accompanying a person's lack of forgiveness:

> Then his master, after he had called him, said to him, "You wicked servant! I forgave you all that debt because you begged me. Should you not also have had compassion on your fellow servant, just as I had pity on you?"

> And his master was angry, and delivered him to the torturers until he should pay all that was due to him. "So My heavenly Father also will do to you if each of you, from his heart, does not forgive his brother his trespasses."

"From this verse, I believe God will allow all those who refuse to forgive others to be tormented by Satan and his demons, the 'torturers.' This could very well include torment through illness. Another particularly virulent spiritual disease is indifference toward God. When indifference infects a person's heart, it causes the recipient to slowly drift away from Him. The unfortunate victim who contracts this spiritual disease may exhibit the following signs: neglects daily Bible reading or prayer time, decides to watch Sunday football rather than attend church, knowingly engages in activities unacceptable to God, compromises long-held Christian beliefs and values while exchanging them for short-lived sinful pleasure. Eventually, the infected person drifts so far away from God he or she no longer behaves like a Christian. Indifference toward God is dangerous because not only is its progression insidious, it frequently ends in spiritual death."

Lisa thought for a moment and then asked, "What then, Pastor Markham, is your prescription for treating a spiritual disease?"

Smiling at Lisa, Jeremy replied, "God made every human being with an interconnected mind, spirit, and body. A spiritual disease first attacks a person's heart. "In Jeremiah 17:9, we read, 'The heart is deceitful above all things, And desperately wicked; Who can know it?'

"It then metastasizes to the mind and spirit, eventually spreading to the physical body."

A spiritual cure must first heal the heart. With healing of the heart comes healing of the mind, spirit, and body."

Lisa questioned, "Does healing of a spiritual disease always follow in this order?"

"Healing comes," Jeremy replied, "in God's perfect timing and in the order He chooses according to His purpose. Who can comprehend the mind of God or why He allows what He allows when He allows it?"

Steve then posed the question, "How does a person know whether the physical symptoms he or she is experiencing stem from a spiritual disease?"

"In such an instance," Jeremy answered, "One must ask are the standard treatments being used by my physician to treat me successful or unsuccessful? Do my physical symptoms continue to recur? Have the diagnostic tests performed all proved normal? Have consultations with other physicians for additional opinions led to similar conclusions? Are all the doctors involved in my care having a problem diagnosing the cause of my illness? Answers to such questions could help ascertain whether physical symptoms are due to a spiritual disease."

"If it is determined a person has a spiritual illness, what must be done in order to be cured?" Lisa asked. Called to mind were the frequent bouts of abdominal pain she had been experiencing since her parents died.

Pastor Jeremy responded, "A person must take spiritual inventory. He must search deep within his heart, the target of a spiritual disease, and be painfully honest with himself. He must ask God to help him identify a spiritual disease that may be causing physical symptoms. A person must ask: Am I holding a grudge against anyone? Have I failed to forgive someone who has hurt me for no apparent reason? Am I still bitter about my spouse's infidelity? Am I angry at the coworker who received the promotion I deserved? Am I harboring resentment toward the boss who laid me off from my job? Am I participating in activities God would not approve? Am I being disobedient to God by the way I live my life? Am I hiding anger in my heart toward God Himself?

"Any of the spiritual diseases can spread from the heart to the mind and body. Over time, each has the potential to cause physical ailments. So, the various symptoms your patients from Safe Harbor are exhibiting could well be the result of some spiritual disease. If any of the participants left open doors, they are vulnerable to spiritual attack."

Steve commented, "So, this could be the reason Lisa and I are having such a difficult time arriving at a diagnosis. This may be why there is no common thread or symptom. These spiritual diseases are physically attacking each patient differently. Where one may experience abdominal pain or diarrhea, another develops muscle aches or headache. Those unaffected by whatever is happening at Safe Harbor may not have left open doors for the enemy to attack them. Therefore," Steve concluded, "if this outbreak at Safe Harbor is the result of witchcraft and curses, 'A curse without cause shall not alight.'" Appearing enlightened, Steve added, "I think the next step is for Lisa and me to question our patients about disobedience and sin that may be in their lives."

"Remember, Steve," Pastor Jeremy added, "as believers, we have a Great Physician with whom we can consult day or night and by Whose stripes we are healed."

Just then, Lisa began to cry uncontrollably. Through her tears, she sobbed, "I want to see my mom and dad again! I want to hold and kiss them! I want to tell them how much I love and miss them! I'm so angry at God for taking them away from me! I want to see my parents again!" Steve and Pastor Jeremy walked over to Lisa and gently held her.

Jeremy smiled and whispered, "Lisa, you *can* see your mom and dad again. Be healed from the spiritual disease of anger. Repent of the anger and resentment you've harbored in your heart all these years toward God. God had a purpose for taking your parents. We must let God be God, though as human beings we may not always comprehend His ways. He is a loving God, Lisa. He loves you and desires to walk with you through life… all the way into eternity if you allow Him."

Nodding her head and trembling with emotion, Lisa allowed Pastor Markham to lead her in the sinner's prayer. Soon after, Lisa's countenance changed. Joy replaced tears of sadness. The anger bottled up in her heart for so many years seemed to vanish. Lisa's release and spiritual healing had begun. The three rejoiced awhile and then Pastor Jeremy cautioned her. "Remember, God will not be mocked. He knows those who are His and those who are simply playing Christian. Simply reciting the sinner's prayer will not pave the way into heaven for a person. No! No! Absolutely no! Those who truly walk with God obey Him and live according to His commandments. Not only do they confess their sin to God, they repent of it and refuse to ever again engage in the activity. A true believer refuses to compromise God's ways for the ways of the world. Those who are truly God's obey His Word and remain under His wings of protection. They put on the whole armor of God daily thereby enabling them to, as it says in Ephesians 6:16, 'quench all the fiery darts of the wicked one.' They walk with God in faith, believing His every promise 'not giving heed to… fables and commandments of men who turn from the truth,' which is found in Titus 1:14. In 2 Timothy 3:5, we read that a true believer does not live his life, 'having a form of godliness but denying its power.' He refuses to walk with God having lukewarm feet; rather, he walks with feet on fire for Him. In revelation 3:15–17, we read what Jesus says to the Church of the Laodiceans:

"I know your works, that you are neither cold nor hot. I could wish you were cold or hot. So then, because you are lukewarm, and neither cold nor hot, I will vomit you out of My mouth. Because you say, I am rich, have become wealthy, and have need of nothing— and do not know you are wretched, miserable, poor, blind and naked..."

"The Bible also makes it clear in 1 John 2:4, 'He who says, I know Him, and does not keep His commandments, is a liar, and the truth is not in him.' And in Matthew 7:21–23, Jesus gives us this serious warning:

"Not everyone who says to Me, Lord, Lord, shall enter the kingdom of heaven, but he who does the will of My Father in heaven. Many will say to Me in that day, Lord, Lord, have we not prophesied in Your name, cast out demons in Your name, and done many wonders in Your name? And then I will declare to them, depart from Me, you who practice lawlessness!"

"The warning continues in Matthew 8:11–12: 'And I say to you that many will come from east and west, and sit down with Abraham, Isaac, and Jacob in the kingdom of heaven. But the sons of the kingdom will be cast into outer darkness. There will be weeping and gnashing of teeth.'

"And Lisa, believers in Christ stand up for their rights as children of God by taking authority through Jesus' shed blood. They take the kingdom by force, reclaiming from Satan what is rightfully theirs.

They fight through prayer and spiritual warfare." Pastor Markham stopped to catch his breath and then apologized to Steve and Lisa. "I'm sorry if I got carried away. I become impassioned when I speak about the things of God."

"Please do not apologize Pastor Jeremy," Lisa said boldly. "On the contrary, I thank you for all you have imparted tonight. And may God bless you for it!"

By now, it was nine o'clock. Steve and Lisa slowly got up from their chairs and hugged Pastor Markham. Thanking Jeremy once again, they headed back to the hospital. The two doctors were anxious to perform spiritual interviews on their patients. Lisa had entered the Markham residence tormented by long-standing anger, bitterness, resentment, and the accompanying abdominal pain. She left a new woman in Christ, having invited Jesus into her heart as Savior and Lord. Lisa had just been given the "balm of Gilead" that would, henceforth, provide a cure for all her spiritual diseases.

CHAPTER EIGHT

After returning to Clarion General Hospital, Steve and Lisa quickly exited Steve's car and entered the hospital lobby. During the ride back from Jeremy's house, they decided to limit the evening's interviews to three patients because it was late. Choosing Mrs. Chambers, Mr. Holstrom, and Courtney as candidates for the initial interviews, Steve was anxious to learn about their spiritual walks. He wanted to see whether Pastor Markham's witchcraft theory held any validity as to the cause of the Safe Harbor outbreak. Though curious, Lisa was reluctant to actively participate. But, she did want to accompany Steve as an observer. She was interested in listening to what sort of questions he would pose. Afterward, the two would look in on Allison, the sickest of their patients.

Entering the Cardiac Care Unit, Steve and Lisa first went to see Mrs. Chambers. She had been admitted to the hospital from Safe Harbor earlier that day with a myocardial infarction. As they walked into Mrs. Chamber's room, Dr. Talbott noticed an IV containing nitroglycerine flowing into one of her arms and a morphine drip infusing into the other. "Good evening Mrs. Chambers," Steve said, smiling. "How are you feeling tonight?"

"Oh, Dr. Talbott. You must have heard the paramedics brought me back to the hospital. I had a heart attack."

"Yes, Mrs. Chambers," he replied. "Dr. Sommers and I were informed you were admitted to the CCU. We're glad to see that you are resting comfortably."

"My chest pain does seem to have subsided with all the medications they're pumping into me," she responded.

"Mrs. Chambers, do you feel well enough and would you be willing to answer a couple of questions I have regarding your Christian walk?" Steve asked.

"That's a strange request," she said. "But, yes I am willing to answer a few questions. I'm a Christian woman with nothing to hide."

"Thank you Mrs. Chambers." Steve then commenced with the interview. "Romans 3:23 tells us, 'for all have sinned and fall short of the glory of God.' None of us is without sin. To your knowledge, Mrs. Chambers, do you have any unconfessed sin in your life?"

"No, I don't believe so. I mean, none that I can recall," she replied. "I pray to God all the time."

"I'm quite confident that you pray, Mrs. Chambers. But, what I am asking is whether there might be something in your past you are either reluctant or afraid to face? Is it possible you may not have repented of a past sin or failed to ask God to forgive you of it? Or, might you have been deeply hurt by someone, either physically or emotionally, and failed to forgive that person from your heart for injuring you?"

As Mrs. Chambers thought about Steve's questions, large tears began to run down her cheeks. "Throughout my childhood and well into my teenage years," she stated, sobbing, "I was constantly teased and humiliated by classmates because of my weight. I have always been a very large person. I hated those kids for ruining my life and actually prayed that harm would come to them. "I guess I've never truly forgiven them for how mean they were to me."

"Thank you for sharing with us such a painful part of your life," Steve said gently. "Mrs. Chambers, I've posed these questions to you, I guess you can say, as a diagnostic tool. I've learned through my own experience that regardless of whether someone is an avowed Christian, failure to confess sin or to forgive another opens doors for Satan and his minions to enter into that person's life. This, in turn, leads to all sorts of havoc including, I believe, sickness. Jesus tells us in Matthew 18, if we do not forgive another of his trespass against us, God will not forgive us of ours. Further, God will allow the 'torturers' to afflict us until we do decide to forgive. I cannot help but wonder, Mrs. Chambers, whether your heart problem may be related to a satanic attack against you? As a physician, I'm not suggesting there aren't medically proven causes of heart disease, such as poor nutrition, lack of exercise, and stress. But, is it possible all the years of repressed anger and unforgiveness may have given the torturers permission to slowly afflict your body, causing you to, over time, succumb to a heart attack? Is it possible Satan even has the ability, with God's permission, to somehow alter a person's genetics, predisposing him or her to a particular illness?" Steve briefly glanced at Lisa, who appeared very uncomfortable by what he just stated. Steve understood what he had just said to Mrs. Chambers deviated far from the mainstream of contemporary medicine and research.

"Dr. Talbott, I've never really thought about it like that. I have never really applied what Jesus says in Matthew 18 to my own life. I've always considered the passage as being for 'the other guy' rather than me, because I'm a good person."

"It's not about being a good person, Mrs. Chambers. It's about being obedient to what God instructs us to do and how He expects us to live our lives." Steve continued. "The Bible speaks of how people, through sinful behavior and disobedience, can bring bad things upon themselves. But, praise God, if we repent and ask God for His forgiveness, He is quick to forgive. I've often wondered why, after Peter denied Jesus three times, Jesus asked Peter if he loved Him three times? Could it be Jesus was breaking a curse Peter might have brought upon himself for denying Jesus? I don't know. But, it is certainly interesting that Jesus asked Peter the question three times after he denied Jesus three times. Is it possible, then, you may have brought harm upon yourself by not forgiving those kids or by praying that harm would come to them?"

"I just don't know," Mrs. Chambers replied.

"Mrs. Chambers, are you willing to forgive those kids for what they may have done to you so many years ago? And are you willing to repent of the sin of failing to forgive them so God will forgive you?"

"Yes," she sobbed.

"Will you allow me to pray with you right now to break any curses that may have befallen you and pray also for your healing?"

"Yes, I will," she replied. Taking her hand, Steve led Mrs. Chambers in heartfelt prayer:

> Father, we come before you with gratitude for all You have done for us. We come before You with humility because of how great You are. We come before You with thanksgiving in our hearts because of what Jesus did for us on the cross at Calvary, by Whose stripes we are healed. We thank You, Lord, for all the provisions You have promised us in Your Word. You alone are our Provider and Healer. Without You, we are nothing and can do nothing. But through Jesus, we can do all things for as You say in Your Word, we can do all things through Christ Who strengthens us. You alone kept Your chosen people, the Israelites, healthy and free of disease for forty years as they wandered through the desert. It was You who kept the first-century Christians healthy before there was modern medicine. And it will be You who, through our faith and trust in You, will keep us healthy when medicine might not be available in the dark days ahead. Now Father, I hold up Mrs. Chambers to You. She asks for forgiveness for all the years of repressed and unconfessed anger she has kept in her heart because of what was done to her by others. She not only asks for forgiveness but, here and now, repents of the sin of failing to forgive others as we are commanded to do in Your Word. We also break any and all curses that may be actively afflicting Mrs. Chambers due to her disobedience and unconfessed sin. We break them in the name of Jesus! We ask You to heal her of the heart disease within her body. And Satan, we now put you on notice. You no longer have legal ground to trespass in

Mrs. Chamber's body. We cast you out, devil, by the power and in the name of Jesus! Be gone from her body, the temple of the living God!"

After repenting and praying for forgiveness, Mrs. Chambers felt a release she was unable to describe. She could not remember feeling so vibrant and renewed. She thanked Steve with a smile and glow on her face. As they walked out of the room, Lisa immediately pulled Steve aside. She asked him how, as a licensed physician, he could suggest to Mrs. Chambers her heart attack might have been caused by anything other than coronary artery disease. Steve replied, "How do we know when we leave open doors for Satan, he and his torturers will not attack our subconscious by suggesting it is acceptable to follow bad eating habits, or cause us to become complacent and forgo exercise, or whatever lies he may choose. Remember, Lisa, the battle is often initiated in the mind. Afflicting our bodies may then be secondary. Only God knows and only what He allows will occur."

"Who is next on our list to interview," Steve then asked. "Mr. Holstrom and Courtney, who are both in ICU," Lisa replied.

"Let's next go see Mr. Holstrom," he said. As they entered Mr. Holstrom's room, Steve and Lisa observed he had been placed on a cardiac monitor and oxygen through a nasal cannula. A drug called Labetalol typewritten on his IV bag was being administered. Its purpose was to help stabilize Mr. Holstrom's dangerously elevated blood pressure so the stroke would not progress and cause permanent paralysis. "Mr. Holstrom, how are you feeling tonight," Steve queried.

"I'm doing much better Dr. Talbott. Thank you for asking."

"Mr. Holstrom, Dr. Sommers and I have come to visit you for a spiritual purpose. Do you feel well enough to share with us where you are spiritually."

"I suppose I can answer a few questions," he replied with some hesitancy.

Steve continued, "It seems as though you are a person who holds to Christian beliefs and enjoys attending summer camp for Christian families."

"That's true," Mr. Holstrom agreed. Steve then asked if Mr. Holstrom had unconfessed sin in his life or had failed to forgive others, just as he asked Mrs. Chambers. He described to Mr. Holstrom all that Pastor Markham preached in his sermon and spoke to him of the consequences for willful disobedience.

Unlike Mrs. Chambers, Mr. Holstrom's response to Steve was both cynical and unrepentant. He eventually admitted he had been involved with several women during his twenty-five year marriage to Mrs. Holstrom. He also admitted to Steve he was currently in an adulterous relationship with his secretary and had no intention of ending it. Mr. Holstrom refused to pray with Steve and respectfully requested he and Lisa leave his room. Steve thanked Mr. Holstrom for his time, and the two immediately left as requested. "I thought he was a Christian," Lisa innocently said, appearing dumbfounded.

"It's far easier to talk the talk than to walk the walk," Steve sadly commented. "It's between Mr. Holstrom and God."

Steve and Lisa walked to the opposite end of the ICU, where Courtney's room was located. She would be their final interview for the evening. As the two physicians entered, they found Courtney sitting up in bed and in good spirits. Her fever and headache were completely gone. "Good evening Courtney," Steve said, smiling.

"Dr. Talbott! Dr. Sommers! Thanks for coming to see me, but why so late?" Courtney asked with a surprised look. "Has anything happened? Is there something wrong with Lizzie?" she nervously inquired.

"No, Courtney," Lisa replied, "everything is just fine."

Steve then asked, "Courtney, would you be willing to answer some questions regarding your walk with the Lord? Your answers could help us to determine the cause of your illness as well as the outbreak at Safe Harbor."

"Of course I'll answer your questions," she replied without hesitation. Steve proceeded to give her the details of Jeremy's sermon and what the Bible teaches about the consequences for disobedience to God. He then inquired if Courtney might have any unconfessed sin in her life, past or present, or failed to forgive anyone who may have harmed her. Somewhat embarrassed, Courtney admitted to her participation in underage drinking while in high school along with occasional use of marijuana. She also confessed to having engaged in premarital sex, through which Lizzie was conceived. Steve prayed with Courtney as he prayed with Mrs. Chambers. Courtney, too, experienced a release and felt a long-standing weight of guilt lift from her very soul.

Before Steve and Lisa left Courtney's room, Lisa mentioned to Courtney that she would soon be discharged from the hospital if her progress continued. Courtney thanked the doctors and asked if she could tell Lizzie the good news. "Absolutely!" Lisa responded. "I'll send her up with one of the pediatric nurses."

After leaving the intensive care unit, Lisa questioned Steve if he believed God would heal all those affected by the outbreak if they confessed their sins and offered forgiveness to others. He remarked, "God has promised to forgive those who forgive others. But, as to whether God will heal those affected by the Safe Harbor outbreak or, in fact, anyone afflicted by disease remains His decision. What happens will be according to His will. Lisa, we have to be cognizant of the fact that it's not about us. It's about God. It's not about what God can do for us but, rather, what we must do for Him. Far too many people forget God is not our servant. We are God's servants, and what is required of us as His servants is obedience."

"I've never thought of it that way," Lisa stated. "I've always figured if a person does something in God's service, God would reward that person."

"The Bible tells us God will not be indebted to anyone," replied Steve. "He certainly does reward us at times. But, just to receive a reward should not be our main reason for being obedient to Him. Our obedience should be out of love for God and to honor Him for who He is."

Steve and Lisa went to look in on Allison. They saw she was sleeping soundly. Lisa ascertained from reading the note Dr. Martin jotted in

Allison's medical record, that her condition had not changed from her last evaluation. "Well then," Steve suggested, "why don't we go home and get some rest. Tomorrow is another day." Lisa nodded. The friends agreed they would meet back in Allison's room at 6 AM. Entering the elevator, Steve pressed the button to go down to the main floor. Being so fatigued, Steve and Lisa failed to notice they got out in the basement. Apparently, Steve pressed B for basement instead of L for the main lobby. The elevator door closed behind them before they realized their mistake. Lisa pressed the call button, so they could ride it back up to the lobby.

While the physicians were waiting for the next elevator, they heard a strange noise coming from one of the storage rooms down the darkened corridor. As the two walked toward the sound, they noticed a light flickering from under the closed door. The sound grew louder as Steve and Lisa approached the room. It was some sort of monotonous chant produced by several muffled voices. Steve whispered to Lisa they should immediately notify security. Quietly walking back to the bank of elevators, Steve picked up the telephone and dialed 700 to reach someone from the hospital security.

"Hospital security," answered Joe Jenkins.

"Mr. Jenkins," Steve whispered, "please come down to the basement right away. Something is going on down here."

"I'll be right there," Jenkins replied, "but, I don't want to make any noise, so I'll be using the stairs. Just wait for me at the stairwell entrance," he instructed.

Within three minutes, Jenkins met them in the basement. He immediately heard the chanting and observed the flickering light from under the door. It was casting an eerie silhouette onto the floor of the darkened hall. "That's the storage room I found Worth snooping in," Jenkins whispered. As the three walked quietly toward the room, Jenkins spotted a shadowy figure in the hallway, crouched against a wall directly across from the storage room. Moving toward the ominous figure, Jenkins grabbed a Taser from his belt. As the group approached, Lisa was the first to recognize him. "Devin," she whispered. "What are you doing down here?"

"Please be quiet and stand back!" he commanded, pulling a gun from the concealed holster beneath his shirt. As Devin kicked open the door, all stood in disbelief. In the room were dozens of candles, with flames flickering back and forth. In the center of the room stood the missing altar, surrounded by five mysterious figures. They were all dressed in black robes, hoods covering their faces. "Hands up!" Devin shouted as he flipped on the light switch. "I'm a federal agent, and you are all under arrest! Remove your robes *now*, so you can be identified."

Slowly, they began to remove their hoods. The first to be identified was James Clayworth. Next, was his wife, Marisa and then Derry White. The fourth person to remove his hood was a hospital security officer who worked with Jenkins. The final hooded individual had to be coaxed with a Taser shot after refusing to comply. As Devin pointed his gun at the robed coven, he asked Jenkins to remove the person's hood. Everyone froze when they saw it was Chief Doyle. "You can all go to hell!" Doyle screeched.

Then Clayworth, with wild eyes and an evil countenance, shouted at the top of his voice, "My father Lucifer hates all you Christians and so do I! Satan comes to kill, steal, and destroy, and so do we!"

Before Clayworth could say another word, Jenkins knocked him to the ground and quickly handcuffed him. By then, Devin's team of federal agents had entered the room and subdued the remaining members of the coven. After the storage room was cleared and the witnesses to the shocking scene regained their composure, Devin explained the situation. "I'm a federal agent, dealing with interstate drug trafficking. I've been monitoring Clayworth and his organization for the past several months. He is one of the kingpins in a group that travels from state to state, recruiting wayward participants into their cult. During our investigation, we've discovered this organization manufactures and sells illegal drugs throughout the United States. I was sent to Clarion to work undercover after our agency was informed by a member of the Clarion Police Department he believed Chief Doyle was involved in some sort of illegal drug activity."

Just then, Sergeant Fleming entered the room. "Devin, what about the chief?" Roger asked.

"You were correct, Roger. Doyle definitely took part in it. And 'soon-to-be' Chief Fleming, thanks for your help," Devin shouted with a victorious smile.

Lisa asked Devin, "Why did Clayworth follow you out of the cafeteria?"

"Because he was trying to recruit me into his cult," Devin answered with a proud grin. "But, Jim was unsuccessful," he laughed.

Then Steve questioned, "Why was Clayworth attacking Allison so viciously with his witchcraft?"

Devin replied, "Clayworth was attempting to infiltrate Safe Harbor. The camp is rife with Christians, whom he could attack with his coven. He specifically targeted Allison because of her grandparents." Devin continued, "We have reason to believe Clayworth murdered Allison's grandparents because of their ministry dedicated to helping people get out of various cults. Allison's grandparents were Mr. and Mrs. Rayburn."

"So the mystery is solved," Lisa stated as she wept from emotion.

"And the outbreak at Safe Harbor appears to have been fully exposed," Steve added as he turned to hug his friend, colleague, and now sister in Christ, Lisa Sommers. And in his spirit, Steve Talbott again heard that familiar Voice speak so clearly from Revelation 22:14, "Blessed are those who do His commandments, that they may have the right to the tree of life, and may enter through the gates into the city."

And Revelation 21:6–8:

> And He said to me, "It is done! I am the Alpha and the Omega, the Beginning and the End. I will give of the fountain of the water of life freely to him who thirsts. He who overcomes shall inherit all things, and I will be his God and he shall be My son. But the cowardly, unbelieving, abominable, murderers, sexually immoral, sorcerers, idolaters, and all liars shall have their part in

the lake which burns with fire and brimstone, which is the second death."

Revelation 22:20 also came to Steve's mind: "He who testifies to these things says, 'Surely I am coming quickly.' Amen. Even so, come Lord Jesus!"

Author's Commentary

Outbreak at Safe Harbor was written as a clarion call to obedience and holy living. As followers of Jesus Christ, we are instructed in 1 Peter 1:15–16,

> ... but as He who called you is holy, you also be holy in all your conduct, because it is written, "Be holy, for I am holy."

God expects us to live our lives in obedience to Him. He knows our heart and every thought. God cannot be fooled and will not be mocked. Why step out from under God's wings of protection through sinful behavior? Why open doors for the devil and his demon horde to torment and to afflict because of disobedience? If a person truly loves the Lord, he or she will not allow self-will to supersede God's will:

> And those who are Christ's have crucified the flesh with its passions and desires. If we live in the Spirit, let us also walk in the Spirit. (Galatians 5:24–25)

> "I say then: Walk in the Spirit, and you shall not fulfill the lust of the flesh." (Galatians 5:16)

Today, we are today witnessing the dollar in rapid decline, worldwide economic instability, increased virulence of microbial organisms, Iranian threats to annihilate Israel, global terrorism, wars and rumors of war—the list goes on and on. Discerning Christians have little doubt we are living in the last of the last days. The sound of hoofbeats becomes louder and louder, as the Four Horsemen of the Apocalypse approach in great fury. With this in mind, does it not seem important to get close to God? Would it not be prudent to deepen our relationship with God by praying without ceasing and living a moral life in obedience to Him? Is it not better to be like the wise virgins and prepare our hearts for the Lord's imminent return? Jesus tells us:

> "Now when these things begin to happen, look up and lift up your heads, because your redemption draws near." (Luke 21:28)

Brothers and sisters, we are called to obedience and to holy living by a Holy God. At any time, all of God's wrath could be unleashed upon the earth. On that day, would you rather be standing under His wings of protection through obedience or tormented by what is soon coming because of willful disobedience? The choice is yours.

Author's Biographical Information

David R. Madenberg was born in Chicago, Illinois. In Chicago, he also attended medical school and performed a residency in emergency medicine. After completing his medical training, Dr. Madenberg moved to Wisconsin, where he has practiced for nearly thirty years. He resides there with his wife, Heidi. His three children—Courtney, Devin, and Joshua—are grown and have embarked on their own adventures. Dr. Madenberg accepted Jesus as his Messiah and Lord in 1983.

Through the years, Dr. Madenberg has served as medical director for several emergency departments in the Milwaukee area. He has taught advanced cardiac life support to physicians and other medical professionals throughout Wisconsin as a member of the American Heart Association Affiliate Faculty. He also serves as an oral board examiner in emergency medicine for the AOBEM.

Dr. Madenberg attended the WCTC Law Enforcement Academy in 2002. After graduating, he served as SWAT team physician for the Walworth County Sheriff's Office.

Since coming to faith, Dr. Madenberg has enjoyed reading books with Christian themes, though with a special interest in biblical prophecy.

Dr. Madenberg's first book, *Jesus, Israel's Messiah?* was published in 1995 by Vantage Press, New York.